NORTHERN APPALACHIA REVIEW

VOLUME 7

CATAMOUNT
PRESS

an imprint of Sunbury Press, Inc.
Mechanicsburg, PA USA

CATAMOUNT
PRESS

an imprint of Sunbury Press, Inc.
Mechanicsburg, PA USA

FIRST CATAMOUNT PRESS EDITION: March 2026

Set in Adobe Garamond.

Publisher's Cataloging-in-Publication Data
Names: PJ Piccirillo, et al.
Title: Northern Appalachia Review Volume 7.
Description: First trade paperback edition. | Mechanicsburg, PA : Catamount Press, 2026.
Summary: An academic literary journal focused on writers from the northern Appalachia region.
Identifiers: ISBN : 979-8-88819-447-8 (softcover).
Subjects: FICTION / Anthologies | LITERARY COLLECTIONS / American / General | FICTION / Cultural Heritage | POETRY / American / General.

Designed in the USA
0 1 1 2 3 5 8 13 21 34 55

For the Love of Books!

Northern Appalachia Review

The Northern Appalachia Review publishes once annually. U.S. subscription rate is $20 for one copy. See submissions guidelines at NorthernAppReview.com. Address all correspondence to The Editors, generalinquiries@NorthernAppReview.com.

Legacy

Keep
that. It can
be used for tying
that bundle of last month's
Daily News or that stack of
unsolicited credit card applications.

Keep
those. Plastic
drink bottles become
watering vessels for
begonias, car radiators,
or the long leg of a journey.

Keep
those. They
just might save trips
to hardware stores.
Folks are always losing
screws, bolts, and nuts that
keep important stuff from falling apart.

Keep
those broken
toasters, kitchen mixers,
portable drills, saws, and drivers
in a pasteboard box on the back porch,
until they spill over to another box, the back
yard, the front porch and then the steps. Until

they creep stealthily under the leafy crepe myrtles
that yield their secret hoards to the cold hands of winter.

When a daughter or a sibling or a neighbor casts a questioning eye
on what appears to be rubble and wreckage leading to my unlocked
    door
I will answer that those leavings that wrap round me
like a coverlet of keepings are simply
the evidence of living.

What Do Widows Do in Cemeteries?

There is no instruction manual for cemetery visits.

When you buried your husband, the woods behind the grave stood several feet away. Now, persistent evergreens encroach so close to the granite marker that you trim them back.

And then what?

Do you gaze at his headstone, like a person struck into stone herself? Do you talk to him? Ask him if he felt all right when he left on the bicycle that morning? Question what he meant by *I overdid it today* moments before he collapsed? Tell him you sometimes hug the teddy bear made from his favorite sweatshirt and ski hat? Report that his niece, whom he would remember as a middle school *Nutcracker* dancer, lives and works in Chicago now? That his nephew, playing his second year of high school baseball, has a great throwing arm? Say how much you wish he could have gone to Ireland with you? Pull up photos of Galway Cathedral, the place where you felt his presence, and hold the phone up to his name carved in granite, as if he still could see such things?

Generations of widows have preceded you. Aunts and great aunts. Cousins. Grandmothers. Your mother. His mother. Not a single widow in your family has remarried. They must have been experts at this. What did they do in cemeteries?

The same things as you? Unload the car filled with spray cleaner, scrub brush, pruning shears, trowel, gallons of water, and maybe some flowers to plant? Scrub dirt off the stone's carving, even as you remember the dust coating his basement workbench where he carefully attended to shiny bicycle gadgets but never cleaned the surface he worked on? Busy yourself pulling weeds? Pretty the plot with perennials that he wouldn't care about— deer-resistant black-eyed susans and lavender? Do you—did those other widows—do these things because physical activity relieves the emptiness?

Or do you—did they—perform these graveside rites because your name is on the headstone too, with no end date? That blank space is nearly shouting that you are moving on without him, highlighting that you have sold his guitars and bicycles, that you have traveled to places he, too, would have loved, that you have redone his cement block basement lair with drywall painted sunshine yellow and added a rocking chair and an electric heater made to look like a fireplace.

Is this what widows do in cemeteries? You want to ask those other widows, but they, too, are gone. Did they, like you, prattle on about family? Log events their husbands missed? Clean granite and weed flowers? Did they ever feel the weight you sometimes feel? Full of guilt over whether you did enough on that awful day when he collapsed? Should you—could you—have immediately insisted that he lie down when he talked about overdoing it? Known more about proper CPR? Could you have prevented the sudden end of heartbeats?

Before you leave, you walk downhill and survey the line of stones marking the widows you knew. *What now?* You ask them. *Is there an absolution for living on?*

Bright pink catches your eye as you reach the headstones. The fading petals of the peony that one of the widows planted decades ago on your family's plot. The peony that survives northwestern Pennsylvania's winter snow and cold and bursts out in bright color anew each spring.

As you stand beside the other widows' graves, you imagine hearing the keystrokes of your mother's typewriter as she prepared the minutes for the local Senior Center. The group she found purpose in after your father died. You recall your grandmother making toast and silver tea for eight-year-old you in her kitchen, empty of the grandfather who died long before you were born. Your eye falls on the marker of an aunt, the only widow who seemed lost after her husband died. Needy. Clingy. Without interests of her own.

Does anyone know what to do in cemeteries? Are there ways to balance the past and the future? After a decade, you're still not sure. Maybe the other widows weren't either. Yet you easily identify those who thrived in widowhood. Has their message been waiting for you all this time?

To imitate the peony? To emerge from each of life's hard seasons and unfurl your magenta petals.

Don't Come for Me, Mr. Death

You've been picking and picking
At my mind, tongue, and skin
Since Lord knows when on this Good Earth
You've been salvaging my departed strands
Left in sinks or on throw pillows for your handbasket
Slowly collecting parts of me for your weaving
Scraping off dry skin during my sleeping
Gathering remains from my womb in bedsheets
I can witness your oh-so sly handy work
Letting my drooping body sour more
Until my collard greens are tasteless like gravestones
My fingertips numb like bloated corpses
My posture curves more than country roads
Then you trick my words to become Russian roulette
While my eyesight remains a chance at bingo
I say in plain daylight, *Don't come for me, Mister!*
Not when Saint Peter's keys are gone missing
And the whole world's marching on Hell Street

Easter Sunday

I don my gloves, fetch
my bag, brain-gray
with a navy Food Lion
logo. Beside the road,

I find the butts—
2 Marlboro Lights, 1 Pall Mall,
3 unidentifiable, shredding
to white and yellow fluff.

1 styrofoam clamshell
& its accompanying checkered
liner floating nearby—both
fill my sack alongside paper

napkins, a glossy red Purina dog
treat pouch, an airplane bottle
devoid of its liquid contents,
the white and yellow Bojangles bag.

I see my neighbors don their suits
& dresses patterned with purple flowers
like the ones at my feet. These folks
are headed to church; I am already there.

Pokeweed Woman

You were pokeroot, shriveled and starving
as an autumn shrub, and you taught mountain women

to eat. They learned to harvest spring leaves with thin fingers,
boil your body's purple stems before poison could take them.

So, they decided to change you; you, that violent, hovering plant,
became an altar for their fingernails and filthy hair

in place of every plucked leaf. When a woman would die,
you kept her bones at your roots until you could stand

like she did. Unsteady on the mudthick mountainside,
others taught you womanhood. You learned to survive

by splitting berry from seed—that delicate death,
once belonging only to you—until your new hands were more red

stain than skin. Hungry hill woman, you were the sepal
of life and everything after. Berry blood is no different from yours.

Naamah Speaks

"I'm going to destroy all flesh because the world
is too full of violence," says God. No irony there.
My husband hammers together gopherwood
and sets traps, luring animals that crowd our house
with brays and hisses, growls and whines and barnyard smells
while he puffs with self-importance as if he and he alone
can save the world.

And what about me? I doubt you know my name.
Historians will someday suggest 103 possibilities.
My job? To cull seeds. God scolds me for balking
at the cantaloupe, that obnoxious, overpowering
fruit that dominates fruit salads until all the others
taste just like it. And really? I protest.
Invasive honeysuckle, kudzu, multiflora rose?
When God gets pissed, I say, and dandelions?
That one's reverse psychology, and God falls
right into my trap, cursing my disobedience,
vowing that because of me, dandelions will forever cover
the earth. I glare and pout, but I'm smiling inside.

For 371 days of rain, it's the image of flowers I cling
to, of leaving behind giraffes that smell like poo, colonies
of cockroaches, rats and hyenas and platypuses, horned lizards
and horseshoe bats, the mildew-scented feet of my sons and husband.
I'll alight into fields of miniature suns. The manes of ferocious cats.
Threads of gold like the ones I wove through my hair as a girl. Later
puffs of light, white as the moon that lifts the tides. White
as the hair of the old lady I am now, flying away in a breath,

in a wish, in a scattering of the stars by which we navigate,
like our fragile lives: those flowers will commemorate me
though you'll never know my name.

Immaculate Heart

Her maxi pad soaked again with thick clots of dark blood, Sister Philomena Moriarty goes to the restroom between the entrée (grilled Pacific salmon on mixed greens) and the cake (raspberry filled with buttercream frosting) while the bridal shower guests settle into a mimosa-induced complacency and the wait staff tries simultaneously to clear seventy-five luncheon plates, serve the dessert course, replenish white wine, and field requests for coffee.

In the last stall at the far end of the ladies' room at Highview Country Club, Sister Phil encloses herself. She hangs her purse on the hook inside the louvered plantation door and touches the back of her dress with her fingertips to check for leakage.

The older Sisters have a spirituality of perimenopause. They say that "the curse of Eve" gets heavier before it dissipates, just as the middle years of religious life can feel more burdensome, like a crisis of faith before the contented latter stage of convent living.

The only member of her congregation who still menstruates, Sister Phil looks forward to the change of life, the drying up of her unused womb. Five years ago, when she was thirty-seven, a gynecologist performing an annual exam had exclaimed with surprise, "Your hymen is still intact! Would you like me to break it for you?" Sister Phil has never had vaginal intercourse, has never even used a tampon. In that exam room, wearing nothing but a paper gown, she had been both pleased at the official validation of her virginity and offended at the implication that medical science would treat it.

The ladies' lounge still has the green toile wallpaper that Sister Phil loved as a child. Waiting for her mother or one of her aunts, Philomena—called Minnie back then—used to lie across a round velvet pouffe in the outer lounge area and study the toile images of women in Victorian dresses sitting in the grass, holding china teacups and gossiping merrily;

young couples dancing outdoors, leaping and twirling chastely, never touching; girls holding up voluminous skirts, revealing dainty ankles and slippered feet while terriers on two legs nipped at the air beside them.

She would follow the repetitions in the paper as her mind completed the pattern around the corner and behind the mirror of the wooden vanity while the wives and daughters of club members freshened their lipstick or powdered their foreheads before re-entering the main dining room or the mixed grill. Even when the fixtures—the old, two-handle pedestal sinks—were upgraded, replaced with a long green marble countertop and slick touchless faucets, the paper stayed intact: creamy, thick, timeless—part of the immutable Highview Country Club code. August and prestigious, the club has remained steadfast for generations of venerable Pittsburgh families.

Pulling up her blue dress and pulling down her tan stockings, Phil checks to make sure no blood has leaked onto her panties. She folds her tall frame onto the low seat, her ankles creaky from years of field hockey.

Wrapping her used maxi pad in layers of toilet paper, she hears young voices and clicking heels—a rush of energy on the other side of the door.

"Oh my God, Haley, this is sooo fancy. You've made it, girl!" one says.

"Yeah. I'm gonna stay friends with you. Must be nice to be this rich," says another. "Bring me back to your club anytime, bruh."

Sister Phil sits perfectly still. Doors open and close down the row. Pee rushes into porcelain. A toilet flushes. Faucets run. Haley laughs with the bridesmaids—her college sorority sisters—all wearing scandalously short dresses and high-strappy sandals, bare-legged and spray-tanned on this cool but sunny April day.

"But, ohmigod, that prayer before we ate—it was so intense," one says. "Is Charlie's aunt an actual nun?"

"Oh, that's his cousin," she hears Haley reply casually. "She's the one who has been on us like every week about getting some bishop to bless our marriage or something. I'm like, what-ever."

Phil pictures Haley, conspicuously braless, in the white lace halter dress that barely covers her rear end, her smooth skin, and her dainty

French manicure. She has long curls arranged over her bare shoulders. Haley is tiny and slim, like a little doll, with brown eyes and very white teeth. Each month, her hair is colored a lighter blond, as if to gradually bleach away her middle-class roots on her way to marrying Charlie.

"She must be like six feet tall, though," one of the girls comments. "I mean, she's like freakishly tall." Phil thinks this voice belongs to the maid of honor *(Alex? Alexa?)*.

"Why does she wear that blue veil?" another demands. "I've never seen a nun look like that."

"I don't know," Haley answers. "She just got back from Haiti or somewhere. I guess that's what they made them wear. She's like a missionary or something."

"His Aunt Rose is obviously super Catholic. Doesn't he have a priest in his family, too?"

"Yeah," says Haley. "That's his uncle, his dad's younger brother. I know. It's a lot."

"I mean, Charlie's family is sooo Catholic," Alex/Alexa says. "Is *he* that Catholic?"

Haley laughs.

Sister Phil's forearms rest on her thighs. Her feet start to tingle. She pictures these girls, carelessly self-indulgent, carefully packaged, leaning over the marble counter to look in the mirror, pouting as they apply fresh gloss.

"He is now," Haley says, "but he won't be for long!" She sounds breezy, ebullient.

Sister Phil looks at the wallpaper, at a couple in front of a snug little house, a rooster standing erect on the fence post with its chest puffed out and its tail feathers spread elegantly. When she was a little girl, she named him Eggbert. She used to imagine him crowing to waken the dancers and the farmers.

They always spent the New Year holiday at the family compound in Florida. The year she was fifteen, one of her older brothers caught her kissing a girl behind the ice cream shop in town. "My God. You are disgusting," he told her.

That night, after dinner at the club, her mother gave her father a "don't blame me" look. Her father said, "Go on ahead, everyone. I want to talk to Minnie."

Her older brothers, in navy Brooks Brothers blazers, their blond hair neatly trimmed over their ears and longer on top, sauntered out with their mother while Minnie sat alone at the table with their father. From the doorway, Tommy turned around and smirked at her, and she knew he had told. Their father, Paul Moriarty III, was a busy investment banker, and she rarely enjoyed the privilege of his undivided attention. He put three fingers inside his collar, in unconscious acknowledgment of its tightness, then straightened his tie. On Sundays through Fridays, even in Florida, he wore white dress shirts with French cuffs, a linen suit the only concession to the warm weather. He sipped his Jameson's and waited for the staff to disappear. When the kitchen door swung open and closed, she could hear the laughter of the waiters and cooks on the other side enjoying some kind of inside joke. She stared out the window at the putting green and the ocean beyond. The sun was going down over the water in a symphony of pinks and oranges.

"Minnie, listen to me. I'm only going to say this once," her father told her sternly, looking not in her eyes but at the top of her head. "Your brother told me what happened today. You made a mistake." He paused, cleared his throat uncomfortably. "It was not your fault. Someone tried to lead you down the wrong path." He stopped again, took another sip of his whiskey and held the glass up to the light from the window. "I want to be very, very clear. You must be extremely careful about whom you associate with. You will never bring shame on our family the way you did today." He took a last sip, set the glass down, and stood, summarily.

"Yes, Daddy," she answered meekly. On the table in front of her, in a glass dish on a saucer with a doily, the ice cream with sprinkles slowly melted. Colored candies bled into thick white liquid.

Sister Phil waits for the click of heels and whoosh of the door before emerging from the bathroom stall. As she washes her hands, she stares at her image in the mirror—her pale hair in two neat wings in front of her veil, the freckles across her nose faded by a Pittsburgh winter.

From the ladies' room, she walks through the foyer, goes out the front door, and strides down the sidewalk past the pro shop to a little phone booth, a relic from an earlier era, which sits across from the bench that the golfers use to lace their shoes.

Val answers in a rushed, hushed voice. "Sister Valerie here. How can I help you?"

"What are you doing?" asks Phil. "Are you doing something?"

"I'm at a meeting with the first Communion parents. What's up? Is this important?"

"I just wanted your advice about something. If you have time."

"Can we talk later?"

"I thought it might be better to call you from the club." Phil cradles the phone on her left shoulder and cups her left elbow in her right hand.

Val sighs. "What's up?"

"I'm worried about Charlie," Phil says. She tries to put some urgency in her voice. "I think his fiancée is a corrupting influence."

"So what are you going to do about it? Go to your Auntie?"

Phil can't tell if Val is being sarcastic. She sees a group coming around the pro shop and heading to the men's grill: her father, her brothers, her uncles, her cousins—all the men whose wives and daughters are in the dining room at the shower. She holds the phone and nods sincerely and professionally to give the impression that she is conducting official "church business."

"Yes," she says automatically to cover her confusion. "Yes, I think so."

Phil can tell by the restless posture of the men, by the undercurrent of annoyance in their loud jocularity, that the golf has been unsatisfactory. Phil's brother, Paul IV, sees her in the phone booth and rolls his eyes, tilting his head toward Haley's father, Andy, whom Phil understands to be a less-than-competent golfer. For lunch in the men's grill, where a sport coat is not required, the Moriarty men are wearing bright, pastel polo shirts made of technical fabrics, emblazoned with the names of clubs of other exclusive resorts, such as Doral, Pebble Beach, and Pinehurst. Thrilled to be playing with his daughter's future in-laws, Andy smiles broadly. He is wearing an IC Light baseball cap and a blue and white, striped cotton polo shirt which is soaked under the armpits even on this relatively cool day..

Phil watches the men file past and lifts her hand in benediction to them.

"Well, I guess that's it then," says Val. "Good luck with it. I need to get back to my meeting."

* * *

On top of a hill in an established suburb north of Pittsburgh, Highview's clubhouse has panoramic views of the city. The dining room has floor-to-ceiling windows that overlook the golf course. Crystal chandeliers with sparkling glass pendants gleam above the parquet floor.

While the men played golf on this early spring day, the women and girls—aunts, sisters, cousins, friends—had gone to early-morning hair appointments. Afterward, dressed in expensive florals from designers' spring lines, they bore lavish gifts to the shower. Everyone knows that the ritual bestowing of kitchen appliances and household textiles provides only a pretext for the real theatrics: assessing how the bride-to-be measures up to the Moriarty women.

Rose Moriarty, the unmarried and childless matriarch of one of Pittsburgh's wealthiest and most pious families—with her cloud of hair like a white halo—resembles Queen Elizabeth the Second, especially here in her light blue shantung skirt suit and pale stockings (*her legs surprisingly shapely for a woman in her seventies,* Sister Phil thinks). The eldest Moriarty sibling, Rose controls the family trust with an iron fist, insisting on strict adherence to the conservative Catholic values that she understands as her parents' legacy—even as much as the billions in land and assets left for their descendants. Rose's six younger brothers, all bankers and lawyers, compete for her good graces, given the discretionary nature of that trust. To a man, they enjoy the blessing of their generous allowances. They appreciate the club memberships, the connections, and the annual ski trips to Jackson Hole. They belong to the Patronage Society, the association for high net-worth Catholics who, according to their covenant, "defend their faith with courage and conviction in their homes and workplaces." The youngest Moriarty brother, Father Michael, is both a diocesan priest and the chaplain of the society. The sisters-in-law, slender and pretty, have expensive hair in conforming shades of blond and tasteful wardrobes. They sit on the boards at the Children's Hospital, the Museum of Art, and the Catholic Charities. Phil's mother, Anne, never eats carbs and golfs four times a week—at Highview in the summer and at the club in Naples in the winter.

Rose has thirty-seven nieces and nephews, but Phil—the oldest girl, the tomboy niece who took the veil—is her favorite. Phil's parents had not been thrilled with her decision to join the Visitation Sisters. "But it's better than the alternative," her mother had said, looking significantly at her father. Aunt Rose, on the other hand, was delighted. Two of her aunts were Sisters of Mercy. In a well-populated family, the occasional celibacy attests to a kind of collective piety.

"Why didn't you ever get married, Aunt Rose?" fourteen-year-old Phil had asked.

"God had other plans for me, Philomena."

"What plans?" she persisted. "What did God want you to do?"

"My father worked incredibly hard for this family, building up the business that his father started. But he always said that just as much credit went to my mother. She died when I was fifteen, but I still remember her going to Mass every day and saying the rosary every night. My father told me that his mother was the same way. A good Catholic. A daily communicant." Rose paused. She looked at her niece with perceptive, blue eyes. "He said my grandfather never would have made such a fortune without my grandmother's prayers. And that he wouldn't have done so well without my mother's."

"So God wanted you to pray?"

"One thing I know for sure, as long as our family has been faithful, we have been blessed by God."

Covered with floor-length white linens, the banquet tables in front of the window are decorated with silver-framed photos of Haley and Charlie: drinking wine on a rooftop bar, playing at a beach (Haley in a white bikini), dancing in Mexico (wearing sombreros), laughing at a

Steelers game (in black and gold jerseys), and skiing in Utah. Walking past the display on her return from the ladies' room, Phil feels how horrified Aunt Rose must be. Fifteen years ago, when Phil was their age, couples did not flaunt their pre-marital promiscuity like this.

The tables are piled high with gifts, but opening them will not be part of the day's festivities. Exclaiming over so many presents would be both unbearably time-consuming and indecorous for a Moriarty—or a soon-to-be. The spoils of the day will be whisked away to the groom's house and unwrapped privately. Earlier, Sister Phil overheard Charlie's mother, Aunt Judy, hinting that Haley already lives there with Charlie, but no one mentions this fact publicly, lest Rose find out—still two months until the wedding.

A cardinal hops on the sidewalk outside the window. Daffodils waver bravely in the spring wind.

As Phil makes her way to the head table, Karen, the bride's mother, stands to intercept her. Karen wears a skirt suit in the shade of peach that Haley has chosen as her wedding color. The skirt pulls taut across her soft stomach, and the jacket looks rumpled. Karen works as a technician at the mammography center. *She squeezes boobies all day long,* thinks Phil. She has to grab them and press them flat into the machine that takes pictures of breast tissue and looks for suspicious growth. The machine turning, Karen squeezing the exposed flesh of strangers, over and over, all day long. Sister Phil can tell that Karen has had too many mimosas. At the same time, she suddenly realizes that she is closer in age to her cousin's future mother-in-law than she is to Haley and Charlie, and she experiences a moment of vertigo, not knowing to which generation she belongs.

Karen takes Sister Phil's hand in her own and says, "Thank you for that beautiful prayer. Having you here was almost as good as having a priest."

Sister Phil smiles thinly. "Thank you," she says.

Karen drops Phil's hand and touches one of the presents—a soft, white bulgy package with the recognizable Neiman Marcus logo. *Probably king-size sheets, judging by the size of the package,* Phil thinks. She has seen the bedding on the bridal registry. When she sleeps at her parents' house, she sleeps on Italian cotton sheets in a Queen bed. At the convent, she has been accustomed to a lower thread count and a narrower bed.

Karen says, "All these gifts. My little girl is so lucky to be joining this family."

Phil nods noncommittally. "In our family, the holy sacrament of marriage is very precious," she says.

"Everyone is just so kind," Karen continues. "We really feel blessed."

Sister Phil thinks about Haley trying to make Charlie less Catholic. She thinks of them living together in Charlie's house, sleeping in the same bed before their wedding. On their gift registry, they asked for contributions to their "honeymoon fund."

Phil looks down at Karen, short, like Haley, and wearing flats. "I would advise Haley not to open anything yet," says Phil. "Given the possibility that things would have to be returned. Better to leave them in the original packaging." She smiles at Karen with her mouth closed and moves away.

Sister Phil takes her seat next to Aunt Rose at the table with her mother, Aunt Judy, and some of the other aunts. The servers pass out slices of cake and pour coffee from silver pots into china cups with rattling saucers.

Karen, still standing next to the gift table, looks confused and slightly drunk. While the aunts discuss whether the holy hour before the wedding should take place on Friday evening or Saturday morning, Phil leans toward Aunt Rose and begins, "I think you need to know something about Haley."

Rose stands a few minutes later, a displeased expression on her face. "Please excuse me," she tells the others. While the shower guests eat their cake, Rose walks to the wide hallway outside the dining room, with the fox hunting oil paintings on the walls. Her black leather pumps sink noiselessly into the thick carpet. The head waiter comes over to attend to her.

"Ms. Moriarty, what can I do for you?"

"Randy, please fetch my brothers, Paul and Skip. I'd like to speak to them both in the library."

"Of course, Ms. Moriarty. I'll let them know right away."

By the time Rose returns to the dining room, the china plates with cake crumbs and globs of buttercream frosting have been mostly shoved aside. Peach tulips in thick bunches on each table are starting to sag. A kind of sugary torpor has descended on the room.

As the de facto hostess, Aunt Rose goes to stand in the center of the room and clears her throat gently. The serving staff steps backward to fade against the walls.

"I want to thank you all for coming today, to join with our family as we celebrate dear Charles and Haley." She pulls herself up to her full height and looks around the room at the assembled guests. Her gaze rests for a moment on Phil, and she nods.

"At this time, I would like to ask my niece, Sister Philomena Moriarty, to give a final blessing to this gathering."

Phil rises. She is conscious of the impression she makes in her blue dress and veil: tall and ungainly, but, also, modest and holy.

In Haiti, Sister Phil had lived in a small house with Sister Val, her partner in ministry. They ran after-school and summer programs for the children of the parish, teaching them English and preparing them for the sacraments of reconciliation and first Communion, loving their beautiful brown skin and enchanting smiles.

The mothers and fathers of those children treated Sister Phil and Sister Val with deference. They came to the mission center for catechism classes, for rosaries, and for holy days. They never had schedule conflicts or seemed in a hurry to leave. They appreciated the gifts from the mission (clothing or bags of rice) and repeated over and over, "Mèsi anpil, Sè!" They prayed loudly, and they sang the hymns with vigor. The Haitians loved Jesus and the Church in a way that Sister Phil had never seen in Pittsburgh.

Mother Luke had sent Sister Phil and Sister Val to Haiti together with the understanding that they would be discreet about their partnership. Now that they are both back in the US—the situation in Haiti making the ministry impossible for foreign sisters, Mother Luke had sent Val to Florida to do parish work with Haitian immigrants. She called Phil back to Pittsburgh to wait for her next assignment. Phil aches with homesickness for the tropical air—aches with loneliness for Val who played her guitar and sang "Rejouis-toi Marie" in a wavery soprano. Phil and Val loved all the same songs.

"Heavenly Father," Sister Phil begins to pray. "We thank you for the gifts of life and of love. We thank you for letting us know you and giving us opportunities to serve you." She pauses. She looks around the room. "We thank you for this nourishing meal, for the hands that prepared and served it, for the time together, for the opportunity to learn about one another." She looks at Haley and smiles beatifically. "We pray that we might make ourselves worthy of the gifts you have given us by living lives of purity." She looks down. "Please bless those who are hungry, those who are alone, and those who long for a closer relationship with you. Amen."

On a table near the door, seventy-five gift bags for the guests were tagged with a heart-shaped cardstock photo of the bride and groom raising glasses of champagne, Haley's diamond engagement ring flashing on her left hand. On the other side, handwritten notes say, "We can't wait to celebrate our wedding day with you! xoxo Haley and Charlie." The bags contain full-size bottles of an expensive French lotion, soy candles in glass jars, white rosaries, and individually packaged cookies shaped like a wedding dress and decorated with royal icing and pearly nonpareils.

The guests cluster around the table to collect their party favors. Haley and her mother stand with Judy, handing a gift bag to each departing guest, repeating, "Thank you so much" and "It was so nice meeting you" over and over again.

Phil will take any leftover gift bags back to the convent, along with the leftover cake. The Sisters will gush over the treats. They appreciate the generosity of the Moriarty family.

After the guests have mostly gone and the little girls in the family, released from the strictness of the formal proceedings, start a game of chase down the hallway to the coat closet, Sister Phil looks outside.

She sees Charlie on the balcony with Haley. She can tell by his posture that Uncle Skip will have talked to him by now—conveyed the imperative. The day is lovely, one of those early spring days that smells like mulch and hyacinths.

Charlie wears a navy Highview golf shirt with belted shorts. Leather loafers without socks. He has the thickening waist of a pampered young man with an office job. The back of his neck is sunburned from his morning of golf.

Haley stands barefoot on the concrete patio, holding her ridiculously high-strapped sandals in her left hand. She barely comes up to Charlie's shoulder.

The patio extends out from the back of the building and has a half-circle railing around a platform that overlooks the valley. It's a favorite spot for couples to take wedding photos.

Sister Phil cannot tell what they are saying to one another. Charlie looks downcast. His hands in his pockets, he kicks the ground petulantly.

Haley appears to be telling him something emphatically.

They stand apart, stiffly, like two dancing figures in toile, bobbing up and down at arm's length but never coming close enough to touch, as if following some courtship convention from a more formal civilization.

White Witch of Moss Creek

In Memory of Ann Hudak

Mrs. Hudak summoned me next door
innumerable times: *Come here, Honey, will ya?*
Mud-pie dirty, shaking a bit from eagerness
to please, or hearing in my head the warning
not to tell our business ever, I'd lean
against her belly, grab a bunch of house dress
for support, let her wipe my face with her hem.
There now. See how pretty? Yes, Sugar, yes.
Croons soft as cream, incantatory, fed an ache;
hands calloused but gentle cupped and steadied
mine, pressed in one a shiny nickel.

A pound of minced ham, okay? A loaf of bread,
and tell Agnes put it on the new two weeks.
(a measured, rhythmic pace I later learned
we use on high-strung children, or some
luckless witness who, stunned insensible
had faith been kind, stays keenly conscious).
She held my eyes with hers (*I see you!*) then
let me go to seek in errands a self beyond
the smoking dumps of boney.
Touched by magic, I bowed to portals,
washhouse, giddy with belief, and glimpsed
behind the company store a castle's shadow.

But that was long ago, some forty years.
Last spring, her son, her daughters—noble

grieving masks—received her tributes.
I tried to tell her power, how once she caught
me, falling, with her eyes, and sent me
dancing, jeweled, erect to meet my life.
They seemed confused, uncomprehending.
Or, perhaps, they guessed I never told her.
Or, had I read my loss in their faces,
and she no longer here to console me?

      Outside the stars were white as doves
in darkened choir lofts, waiting to sing.

Heart of Stone

Your chafed hands spoke in shadows on the wall,
"A rock is only an unemployed stone."

Hefting the facing stone's grimaced weight,
"If your passion is high, the stones are light."

Gravity kept your artful stones in place,
"Everything is held in place by magic."

On the coping stone you'd wand a hazel stick,
"While I lay down, stay up!"

Whispering in every rock transformed to stone:
"Return me to the earth when my spell is done."

Unthaw

When creek ice thaws,
red-bellied woodpeckers
knock on ash trees,
peel back bark-flesh
to suck out beetles,
larvae, and emerald borers.
Cedar waxwings whistle
alerts mid-migration,

here, here—ripe berries.
Here, here—ripe berries.

With smooth soft-landings,
they flock to hawthorn fruit,
plump and puffed
with sweet syrupy juice
that stains the beak.
Perched among unkempt
bushes along the bank,
blooms despite the frost,
undeterred
by the bite of winter,

they feast
like famished kings.

Ripe berries—here, here.
Ripe berries—here, here.

even least things happen so much

the clink of you making coffee—that and your smile
my reward for leaving a cocoon of blankets

chill morning air waltzes with fog
until sun and oranging leaves warm the day enough

we scuffle through leaves on our favorite trail
—a sound like ruffled skirts curtseying

louder—two hawks in discussion
about who should perch on which reaching tree

a bass note—the low beat of great gray heron wings
as he drags his feet inches above the mirror of pond

a chorus of creaky hinges as a quorum
of blackbirds hold a treetop meeting

seven sparrows flit from bush to tree and back
we walk through their song into a quiet

remember that year we drove miles on country roads
only to find mighty fine fall foliage on our own street?

sunset slides narrow beneath our porch roof
upgrading the neighborhood—now rendered golden

we bemoan the too many streetlights
celebrate random nights when moon stripes our bedcover

Spots

Let's start at this one here, on the river. A houseboat named *Felix Locus*—"happy place," and it is; especially in summer, facing upriver at the end of the marina, an unobstructed mile of the Ohio visible against the background of wooded hills and hidden busy-ness: Lunken airport, Four Seasons marina, a towboat terminal, here and there little coves with fishermen, and all along the Kentucky side, Route 8 sliding stretch by stretch slowly down the hill.

***

Or many, many more miles upriver, the spot my grandfather Ironhead marked with a spill of tar on a rock: secret Hague family fishing place, Dill's Best pipe smoke, driftwood fire, shadows, bats, mayflies, sleek channel cats at midnight; Steubenville, Ohio, where Clark B. Firestone, member of the Literary Club of Cincinnati, began his book *Sycamore Shores* one flood spring long ago. "It was still raining when I embarked at Steubenville, but the leaden skies and turbid waters were at least the portent of a swift and vital journey."

***

Or the stretch of river he'd eventually get to called Long Reach, 17 miles, the longest and straightest reach (meaning, according to the US Geological Survey, "any length of a stream or river . . . used by hydrologists when they're referring to a small section of a stream or river rather than its entire length."). I have driven the Ohio side of it many times in the summer, the blue of aerial perspective thickening the distance. Along its West Virginia shore, Captain Fred Way made a recording of dozens of old steamboat whistles, powered by a big steam line laid along the banks.

***

The spot along the Clear Fork of the Little Muskingum River where, in my post-divorce bachelor wandering days, I walked the creek, fishing for bluegills and rock bass, cigarette hanging from my mouth, hair wild and tangled, my little dog Doubletree Mutt ashore, watching and barking. Maybe one car in an hour, slowly gliding by.

* * *

The spot along that same Little Muskingum, somewhere far below the village of Dart, where my buddies Jim Quinlivan and Bob Collins and I took the canoe out after making our way back upstream following a foray into the Ohio far to the south and east. We forgot one of the extra-broad paddles on the bank—forty dollars gone to jewelweed and the digs of snapping turtles.

* * *

Or the spot at the top of the bluff just upriver from Weirton, West Virginia, and the neatly trimmed private hedge lining the Country Club lawn, Steubenville dimly visible far downriver at a bend, a gray cloud of floating mill smoke.

A photo of the above is on the cover of *Learning How*, my book of stories, yarns, and tales. The quote is from my story, "Big Sandy Afternoon."

One afternoon on the Kentucky shore of the Big Sandy River, just down from a place called Scuffletown Bar and within easy eyeshot of Olive, West Virginia, three gentlemen of the region were engaged in lively conversation over a case of beer. The weather that day was golden: willows trembled in the moderate upriver breeze, schools of perch and shad flashed in the channel, and a young Cooper's Hawk climbed serenely on a steady thermal just to the west of Limestone Knob, which loomed in the hazy distance over the gentlemen's shoulders."

* * *

And the very tight spot way out of one of the distant old haul roads in the coal country near Adena, Ohio, where my dad's station wagon wouldn't start, in which I'd been making out for hours with my girlfriend, already late getting home. That was twenty years before cellphones.

* * *

Not only physical places, but also, as in Wordsworth's *The Prelude*, "spots in time:"
There are in our existence spots of time,
That with distinct pre-eminence retain
A renovating virtue, whence, depressed,
By false opinion and contentious thought,
Or aught of heavier or more deadly weight,
In trivial occupations, and the round
Of ordinary intercourse, our minds
Are nourished and invisibly repaired;
A virtue, by which pleasure is enhanced,
That penetrates, enables us to mount
When high, more high, and lifts us up when fallen.

* * *

Walking along Troublesome Creek, Knott County, Kentucky, below the campus of Hindman Settlement School. A box turtle plods upstream in the shallows, and above him in the opposite direction, a kingfisher streaks in green air downstream. In a tiny spot, they are a dozen feet apart in the same vertical plane, exactly together in one up-and-down time. This is where and when the world, for a moment, stops.

time to

for susan smajda

hang it hang it all up / out / hang the old clothes
cloths gingham kitchen calico stained thoughts
scrap skirt remnants of torn soul-silk do not think
to stitch the ripped hang it up / out / with mom's
pocket flask stashed in that straw bag hang it up
/ out with the caught grown-over stuck straight
copper rod for touch exercises that awaken
fingertips hang the outlived outlined inherited—
tarnished silver rattle your brother paul teethed
on hang it with the variegated unirrigated pressed
petunia petals for love hang it all up on the line
gather each bit into a cloth knot tie the knot with
grandma nina's connecticut pantry twine—even
the pearl precious pieces broken or not knot it
hang it alongside the rusted saw the headless
hammer your father's—workbench basement
tools hung on nails hang it with the imagined the
forgotten the remembered hang it tie it to the last
tilting cross beam of the last slanted weathered
pine—cross at the end of the last dirt road where
the last black crow in-caw flight erases over all
your tall wild blue green corn tasseling grasses in
that first summer field of   burning   red
roses

Amy Le Ann Richardson

The Room Where

It was the spare bedroom in Mamaw's house where she stored Christmas popcorn tins of buttons and Danish cookie tins of thread. I used to sneak in there to eat chocolates from the box of Zachary's I knew she kept in the dresser. Until I was a teenager, and she grew sicker from cancer spreading all over her body, and they moved in a hospital bed to replace the full-sized one, and then, it became her room. Then, it was the room where I'd stand in the doorway and watch my mom beg her to eat, sit by her bed and fall asleep in the chair, and clean her up for visitors. It was the room where I sat at her bedside and witnessed as she took her last breath, gasping, then silence, until everyone else in the room began wailing, and I sneaked out the front door and down the hot asphalt road with bare feet, not noticing until the blisters formed and popped and searing pain pulled me down to the curb where my cousin found me with nothing left but the taste of salt.

Tin Heart

Midsummer Grandma pulled out her kissing
cousins metal dolls, Dutch
kids straining against an afternoon laden

with cream and oven toast. Even
a foot apart, they rushed
to slam faces. She laughed

at their desperation
while my thumbnail dug
into knickered sheen. How

could I sport an ironed
shirt when the cathedral
of a dinner bell

waited for me
to pull its muddy rope, my knees
blitzed sidewalk rough

with hopscotch chalk, rear
dusty from losing
at marbles, aggie tucked into Granny's

knuckles strong against
rainbow stripes. Gravel pressed
into my hams, we rolled the masking

tape into the diamond
of our legs. On the farm
at ten, Grandma told

me kittens drowned
in a bag before her dad
walked out, her mom petrified

on the chintz settee, kids
at the stove scorching milk. Church
be damned, we sang straight

to Jesus from her yellow
couch. Our bodies approximated
heifers and peahens, nothing

special, healed by slathering Vicks
across my bashful
chest. When I sashayed

across the linoleum past the wagon
wheel teacart's hidden drawer, Grandma
turned from slicing deer

liver on gold
flecked Formica—fingers just
blooded—to offer

me the knife.

Physics of Fat

Late-summer sun pushes through the vines, settles
on my concrete porch. An emerald hummingbird attacks
the sugar-water feeder, sideway-glancing
like he's stealing something. He thinks he's getting
away with it. I'm thinking about the weight
I've lost and where it's gone. Does someone else
own it now? Has it wrapped around a new heart?
Or finally filled a D-cup? Mass is always mass
somewhere. My mother would unload fifty pounds
of potatoes through the storm doors, red rusted
metal flung open like a maw, exposing the innards
of our cellar. Balancing burlap bags on sturdy hips. Her work
for my hunger. That was the equation
she knew. She fried and mashed and boiled potential
energy. Her heft now conserved
in my cells. If mass can't be destroyed, something
is always getting bigger. So who has her weight now, after her stomach
was stapled shut? And how do I make sure I don't lose
the parts of her in me? Some women think the phrase is *make ends
    meat.*
Like it's up to them to save fish heads and chicken bones,
wash out organs for stuffing. To boil down carcasses, let fat congeal
    in the pan
and save bacon grease in coffee cans. Some women have a plan
for flesh, for preserving it, making it stretch. The hummingbird
dives in and out of the hedgerow. My neighbor starts the electric
trimmer, tendrils of hawthorn snap and fall. I hope he knows
that those blades can catch hummingbirds on the way back to nests,
full of hatchlings, hungry and growing.

On Jennings Creek

All sorts of terrible things could have happened to Mama since I'd left her at home that morning. She could have gotten up to use the slop jar, taken a fall, and lain on the cold plank floor for hours. Or, she could have misjudged the amount of laudanum she was swallowing—too little and she would suffer those awful pains, too much and she might never wake up. Even though she had insisted that I go to school—said she'd be fine on her own—my conscience had spent the day flogging me senseless. First one out at dismissal, I half-ran, half-walked the mile and a half to the end of Jennings Creek Road and the sorry-looking house Mama and I had to call home.

"Mama!" I called out as I charged through the door. She was in bed as she had promised, but the toast and tea I'd left for her sat untouched, and the slop jar was dry as a bone. "Would you like some fresh tea, Mama? Water? Can I help you up to empty your bladder?"

"No, dear, just the medicine." I pulled the cork from the bottle and steadied her hand as she swallowed. Her head sank gratefully into the pillow.

The evening before, after his visit with Mama, Doc Barnes had gestured that I follow him to his buggy. The groove between his bushy white eyebrows appeared as sunken as the gullies that cut through the hills. "How old are you, Belle?"

"Thirteen last month."

"And the Reverend, has he been back since he left in...."

"December, no, sir."

"But your mother knows where he is? How to reach him?"

He got his answer from my silence. Gaining the buggy seat with effort, he went on, "Bonnie Foster says you've been taking good care of your Mama. See that she takes in fluids, and keep an eye on the chamber pot." He touched his driver's tee lightly to the mare's back, and I watched until his buggy turned from the overgrown lane onto the road.

Bringing my thoughts back to the present, I hustled to the wood box. Once the drafty old house had begun to warm, I returned to Mama's bedside. No doubt about it, she looked a lot worse than she had that morning—lines pinching her mouth, cheeks flushed with fever. I knelt beside her bed. "I'm going to fetch Mrs. Foster, Mama."

To my surprise, her eyes opened. "Wait, Belle. I've been lying here thinking. There are things I need to tell you, things a girl should hear from her mother."

"Don't fret, Mama," I responded, rising to my feet, "you can tell me as soon as I get back."

With that, I hustled into a winter-like evening, not unusual for March—the gurgling of the creek robust. Years ago, Mama had told me that the waters of Jennings Creek flow directly into the Ohio River. The river carries the same waters far south, and then even farther west to the Mississippi. She grew up along the Ohio and watched its traffic—freighters, barges, flatboats, ferries, and passenger boats with names like *Queen Cordelia* and *Sonoma Belle*. That's where she got the idea to name me Belle.

The valley broadened as I neared the Fosters' farm. Close to panic when I passed them earlier, I had paid no attention to the shaggy Angus ruminating their cuds, solemn and thoughtful as old men with tobacco in their cheeks. I had ignored the gnarled apple trees crouching in squat rows as if ashamed of their nakedness and the empty hay fields waiting for April rains to coax them to life. On this shorter jaunt, at least I knew Mama was safely in bed.

Priscilla Foster swung open the door just as I reached the porch of their farmhouse and did her best to look down her nose at me. I guess she'd forgotten who had dragged her through diagramming sentences and interpreting story problems—a tedious task indeed.

"Mama is really sick and—"

That was as far as I got when Priscilla, poised inside the door as though ready to close it, cut me off. "My mama isn't home. She's at a birthing."

The younger Foster daughter, Margaret, peered around her sister, innocent blue eyes reading my distress. She disappeared, and I heard feet pattering and a flute-like voice calling, "Papa!"

A gaunt figure in bib-overalls and bearing the aroma of fresh tobacco opened the door fully. Pipe in hand, he gestured me inside. "Come to the fireside, child, and warm yourself. Priscilla, have Central put a call through to Doc Barnes."

Margaret took one of my hands and led me to the fireplace. I closed my eyes as warmth seeped into my bones. Priscilla passed in a whirl of gingham and stood on a short stool to crank the telephone. Doc, she reported, was also on a call.

Mr. Foster insisted on taking me home, and I followed him to the barn, watching as he hitched up his team—Maud, a mild giant, and Moses, an equally huge and gentle gelding—to the buckboard. He laid a rug across my lap and honored my desire for silence.

Chimney smoke hung heavy as a pall over the roof of the house, and I found Mama fitful, pain dogging her even through the haze of laudanum. I thought of rousing her to take a drink of water but feared she would choke. Mr. Foster tended fires and refilled wood boxes. Before returning home to his chores, he left me with words that served as a mantra: "The missus will be here as soon as she can."

Too exhausted to forage for supper, I stripped to my petticoat and crawled beneath the comforter with Mama. Sleep, however, wanted no part of me, and wakefulness took me back to December and Papa›s unaccountable disappearance. Certain that Mama knew more than she was letting on, I had dogged her with questions: "Where is Papa? Why did he leave? Why didn›t we go with him?" Eventually, I resorted to blaming: "You made him go, didn›t you, Mama? It›s all your fault!"

Used to being ignored by adults, overnight I had become the recipient of secretive stares and whispers; from being just another kid at school, I became a leper. Caught up in my own angst, I gave no thought to how Mama's world had changed. The respect and deference allotted to the pastor's wife fizzled like baking soda when it hits water. The parsonage, the domestic heart of the church, was no longer Mama's bailiwick. If the Fosters hadn't installed us in the ramshackle house at the end of Jennings Creek Road, we'd have been homeless. It took a vicious bout with kidney disease to take Mama down—a wary sort of illness that evaded Doc's and Mrs. Foster's best efforts. But I knew why Mama didn't get better; my drilling and blaming had taken the spirit out of her—so I crammed the whole miserable business into a secret place of my own and went through the motions of surviving.

Well over three months had passed, and I still didn't know when or if Papa would return. A fine-looking man he was, my Papa, a charismatic pastor and favored by the church ladies. The day before he disappeared, Papa had come home half frozen from a funeral far back in the hills, he said. I knew how things would go the minute he came through the door. Anticipating an aromatic kitchen—bread in the oven, a pot of stew on the stove—he found a kitchen bereft of enticing smells and the table strewn with school books and papers, with me lost in my studies. One sweep of his arm cleared the table. Simultaneously, I jumped to salvage my work and produce evidence of a meal in progress.

Meanwhile, Mama shivered on the settee with a warm compress on her belly, a cup of chamomile in her hand, while she fought yet another urinary complaint. Papa ranted. Mama cried. Late that night, a debate, entreaty against demand, resonated all the way upstairs; their headboard pounding against the wall declared the winner. When Papa left the next morning, Mama dropped into a chair at the table, lowered her head onto folded arms, and exhaled as someone whose final obligation had been met. And that was the last we saw of Papa.

As I lay beside Mama, listening to her labored breathing, my final thought before exhaustion shut everything down was a familiar one: *It would be so much easier to pray if it wasn't Papa's face I see when I close my eyes.*

* * *

At Mrs. Foster's urging, Doc Barnes returned the next day and gave Mama enough laudanum to annihilate her pain. "Well, Bonnie," he said,

"I don't know if you've seen this or even heard of it, but our friend Ellen has a ruptured bladder. A rare thing that can happen if the bladder wall's been damaged somehow or compromised from repeated infections. If she was in Boston or New York, things might never have reached this point, but here in the backwoods. . . ."

Turning to me, his voice softened, and he laid a large hand on my shoulder. "I'm afraid your Mama won't be with us much longer, Belle." And with that, he left to tend another patient.

Numb from his diagnosis, I followed Mrs. Foster back to the bed chamber. She dropped into a chair and tossed her voluminous apron over her face, a make-do veil of mourning. I positioned myself at the footboard, hands tight to the railing while leaning into it for support, my focus fixated on the silent figure. I didn't even know I was crying until my hands grew slick against the iron.

Minutes—then maybe an hour, maybe two—passed before my attention suddenly peaked. Mama's deeply sedated body appeared to relax even more, to remit a residual tension. The chest stilled; the features smoothed; a single, long breath made its exit in an audible release through the flaccid mouth.

That was enough to bring Mrs. Foster out of her chair. A small mirror appeared from her pocket and passed beneath the airless nostrils. I heard a heavy sigh and felt insistent fingers peeling mine from the railing. A strong arm grasped me around the waist and urged me through the bedroom door she closed behind us. Had the arm not been there, whatever had overtaken Mama would surely have claimed me too.

A warm, damp cloth materialized and removed the tears and mucus from my hands and face. Then Mrs. Foster sent me to gather all perishables, my clothing, and other needful things. Time passed while my hands obeyed her instructions and hers ministered to Mama. Dark was falling when Mr. Foster appeared in his buckboard. A long, covered conveyance pulled by a team of black horses followed. Mrs. Foster forestalled my climbing into the bed of the wagon, so the three of us crowded into the buckboard seat. The steady feet of Maud and Moses removed me farther and farther from the empty form that had been my mother and the solemn personage who had arrived to care for her final needs.

* * *

Life at the Foster house started out as a blur. All I wanted, at first, was to retreat to the little room under the eaves Mrs. Foster had readied for me and crawl into the bed that smelled of lavender. But I'd been taught better. Mrs. Foster never gave me a list of chores as she did Priscilla, noticing that if I saw something that needed done, I stepped up and did it. Knowing she was keeping an eye on me was actually a comfort.

April eventually brightened the countryside, and I experienced a strange reaction. Anything beautiful—a red sun sinking between the hills, a patch of daffodils popping up overnight—left a weight in my chest, heavy as a brick. One exquisite evening, though, I skipped out after dishes and followed a deer path into the woods.

My solitary walk reminded me of evenings when Papa's church meetings kept him way past dark and Mama could risk a get-away. She would lead me along a path that bordered a dense wood of soldier-straight trunks and opened into a meadow of butterflies and wildflowers beckoning with riotous color. We listened for sleepy chirps and the soft flap of feathered wings tucked away in overhanging branches. There, the encumbrance of parsonage and parishioners, the stricture of demands that nipped always at Mama's heels, eased.

Mama had found another such place—I knew in my heart she had—safe from cruelty and illness. Strangely at peace myself, I returned to the Foster house to Margaret's sweet attachment, Priscilla's snotty undertones, Mrs. Foster's no-nonsense kindness, and Mr. Foster's gentle oversight. On the way back, I found that I could pray again, this time without Papa's face intruding.

* * *

The school year closed in May. Boys were needed for farming, girls for housework. Mrs. Foster crossed her fingers that none of her expectant mothers would go into labor and began to tear the house apart, room by room. Priscilla knew it was useless to complain, and I actually enjoyed removing winter's grime. Shining windows, cobweb-free corners, and winter's bedding flapping on clotheslines lifted my spirits. And it was then, just as I was pinning up the last of the flannel sheets, that I knew I had better get to the privy.

The show of bright red blood against white muslin sent black dots careening before my eyes, and I dropped my head between my knees. Despite the heavy scent of the lime pile in the corner, there was another smell, metallic and menacing; I recognized it all too well from Mama's slop jar when her kidney troubles resulted in bloody urine. Although the sun-baked walls surrounded me, a chill raced up my spine. I'd never bled from *there* before. Never. And Mama was the only person I knew who had. *Could what had happened to Mama be happening to me?* I wondered. My first instinct was to run to Mrs. Foster, but I just couldn't.

The Foster's privy wasn't big on amenities—catalog pages to crumple and a roll of real toilet paper that Priscilla claimed as hers. Making sure no one was watching, I slipped into the yard and skirted a field of timothy grass, beyond which lay a secluded branch of Jennings Creek.

Praying that a random neighbor wasn't trekking along the creek, I slipped out of the soiled drawers and dipped them in the lively stream. The water assumed a pinkish tinge and cleared, resuming its way downstream. I used my teeth to make the first rent in my worn petticoat and tore a couple of wide strips from the bottom. Folded into squares, the make-do padding might offer some protection against a bloody skirt-tail.

Living with the Fosters, I had become accustomed to waking at the rooster's crow and watching the sky brighten through sheer white curtains. But the bleeding forced me out earlier to avoid detection, and, over the next few days, I repeated my process at the creek morning and evening and grew used to donning damp underwear. And then, just as suddenly as the bleeding started, it stopped. There had been no herbal tea, no warm compresses. *Has God healed me? Or will the symptoms return and worsen as Mama's had?* I performed my washing ritual at the creek one last time and rushed back toward the house while questions piled up in my mind.

As I cleared the timothy field, Priscilla stepped out from behind the privy and into my path. "And where have you been?" she asked with a smirk.

I felt my face redden. "None of your business."

"What's that in your hand?" Priscilla made a grab for the roll of damp cotton, and I sidestepped. "Give it to me!" Priscilla's voice rose to a shriek, and she dove again, this time knocking the roll from my grip. She bent and picked up the clothes and the drawers, their pristine whiteness besmirched by the dirt of the path, and her mouth formed a perfect "O" of discovery.

As though it belonged to someone else, my right hand clenched into a fist and landed smack in the middle of Priscilla's face. I saw the blood spurt and heard the unearthly squeal as she lunged. As I felt fingernails tearing down my cheek, I dropped my head and rammed hard into her sternum. We hit the ground rolling. Gaining position on top, I lay spread-eagled across her, pressing down with everything I had.

When she gasped for air, I scrambled to my feet, picked up my cloth pieces, and held them to my cheek. I extended a hand to Priscilla who snuffled through a bloody nose at my feet. I was ready to go face the music when Priscilla reached up. I hoisted her to her feet and handed her the pair of drawers. She hesitated and then began mopping her face. Together we headed toward the house.

Mrs. Foster was standing on the backdoor stoop, hands on hips, Margaret at her heels. "What's this ruckus I hear?" Once she got a good look at us, she breathed, "Good Lord."

"Mama," Priscilla's voice was as nasal as a Frenchman's. "Belle started her flow."

"So," her mother said and followed us inside.

At the kitchen pump, she filled a granite pan and handed us two washing clothes. She pressed along the bridge of Priscilla's nose, inducing another shriek. "I don't think it's broken."

Then she examined my face and clucked over the ugly red stripes. From a shelf above, she took down an ominous-looking brown glass bottle. "This is going to sting, deep as those scratches are. Then we'll see about the other business."

Margaret tugged urgently on her mother's apron. "Mama, what does 'flow' mean?"

A weak spark of optimism began to burn in my brain. Buried beneath the horror of Mama's death lay her words: "There are things I need to tell you, things a girl should hear from her mother." Information about what they called the flow must have been one of those. The first easy breath I'd taken in days filled my chest.

Glowering at me from her side of the wash pan, Priscilla spoke. "I'll never forgive you. I'm six months older and should have started mine first."

Priscilla's hand received a smart slap. "Priscilla Eugenia, for shame."

And I bloodied your face first, too, I thought, squeezing my eyes shut as a good sop of the burning liquid reached my cheek.

* * *

The ringing of the Fosters' phone nearly always meant Mrs. Foster's skill as midwife and expert in female troubles was required, and she never lingered in grabbing her basket and hitching a spirited mare named Millie to her small buggy. One afternoon in June, a tall, skinny boy on a horse of similar build showed up at the Fosters', causing her to order Priscilla to watch Margaret. Then she turned to me. "Come along, Belle."

Millie took us at a brisk trot through the village and entered a trail little wider than a path. Millie slowed of her own accord, and Mrs. Foster gave Millie her head. The trail between huge oaks and elms interlaced with paw-paw and multiflora roses seemed to go on forever. Finally, Mrs. Foster called, "Whoa."

On the far side of a dooryard dense with white clover and harvesting honey bees stood a small house. Instead of a chimney, a long stove pipe stuck through the roof and warm as the day was, smoke poured upward, bearing sparks. "Dear old Frances is likely to burn the place down," Mrs. Foster grumbled as we left Millie and the buggy at a break between clover and a kitchen garden bounded by marigolds. An elderly woman stood at the door, waving a dish towel. We joined her inside.

Through the bedroom door, I could see a girl on a narrow bed, hands clutching a rounded abdomen, hiccuping sobs the only sound. Mrs. Foster led me into the room. "This is Amanda, Belle. Give her your hands." I edged closer, hands extended. The girl gripped them like she'd found a lifeline, and while Mrs. Foster questioned and examined her, a pair of wide blue eyes scrutinized my face.

Mrs. Foster finished and went into the kitchen. "You can douse the fire, Frances. No hot water needed today."

When Mrs. Foster signaled me to join her, I told the girl, "I have to leave now, but maybe I can come back when you have your baby." I had no notion where those words had come from, but the girl loosened her grip and almost smiled.

Millie took us through the forest and between fields of shoulder-high cornstalks. Mrs. Foster gave me a sidelong look, no less intense than a face-to-face scrutiny. "You don't hesitate, do you, Belle? I like that, and I can always use another pair of hands—if you don't mind, that is."

I hadn't felt happy for so long I hardly recognized the surge in my chest. "I'd love to."

* * *

Happiness is always fleeting, especially when the future is uncertain. It had been nearly five months since I'd been bundled onto a buckboard and brought into an established household. No one had mentioned future prospects other than helping with a birthing when Mrs. Foster needed a second pair of hands.

There had been work, seasonal and day-to-day, of which I always did my part. And there were adjustments. Priscilla's flow had arrived in June and created a common ground between us. And Little Margaret found my hair plaiting, wildflower picking, and nursery rhyme telling to her liking. No, it wasn't as if I'd wandered onto the property like a stray, and yet, if the Fosters were to draw the line on hospitality, where would I be shuffled off to?

A couple of weeks after the visit with Frances and Amanda, the tall, skinny boy showed up again on a thoroughly winded horse. Mrs. Foster and I were off into the sunset, the buggy lantern oiled and ready to show us the way home. "Is that boy Amanda's husband?" I asked, holding onto the dashboard.

"Not yet, but before long, I imagine."

"So he's the baby's father."

"No." Her intonation indicated the question-answer period on that topic was over.

One question too absurd to ask was why Priscilla, daughter of the midwife, wasn't already her assistant. Priscilla could barely pluck a chicken without upchucking, and from all I'd heard, giving birth was bloody, painful, and often dangerous. Yet none of that kept me from being as curious as a cat about the workings of a woman's body and wishing there was a way to learn more—and faster.

It couldn't hurt to ask. "How did you learn to be a midwife?"

"Some from helping my mama, but a lot more from Doc. He even gave me a book—way over my head." Her smile was one of fond memories. "You might take a look, though, if you care to."

Manna from heaven, I thought, smiling into the darkening woods that surrounded us.

* * *

In Frances' kitchen, the canning pot held bubbling water. On the table lay a stack of frayed towels, clean and folded. I whisked sweat off my face and pushed up my sleeves the way Mrs. Foster was doing, excitement and fear vying for the upper hand. Together, we scrubbed our hands with lye soap.

"There's more room out here, Frances," Mrs. Foster said, and Amanda's grandmother spread a patched sheet on the table. Between Amanda's contractions, I put an arm around her back, and, with the other hand holding hers, I led her into the kitchen. Lifting her onto the table was a joint effort. The large blue eyes squinted shut as the next contraction hit, and a moan so deep it had to originate in her core accompanied the contraction to its completion.

After that, things escalated quickly. Under the light of two oil lamps and one lantern, Mrs. Foster began to check for the baby's head, and when she said, "It's crowning," she had me loosen my hand from Amanda's grip and place it and its mate high up on her tense abdomen. A strong contraction began. At Mrs. Foster's command, "Push!" Amanda gave it her all, and I shoved on the bulk of her belly steadily and forcefully toward the opening covered with something matted and black. Then the contraction relaxed. But within seconds, another began, and Mrs. Foster was directing us through another push. As though by magic, her hands filled with a tiny human form, an umbilical cord hanging from the belly and an amazing amount of dark hair sticking up from the head.

She cut and knotted the cord, cleared the mouth and nose, and handed the baby to me to wrap in a towel. By that point, Amanda was thoroughly exhausted and unimpressed by her offspring. She gritted her teeth while a final contraction expelled what Mrs. Foster called the afterbirth.

I figured it was all over until I saw blood seeping onto the towel between Amanda's legs. Mrs. Foster bit her lower lip, forehead wrinkling, while her competent hands urgently kneaded the flattened, sagging belly. After a time, her features relaxed, and she gestured for me to see what she'd been doing.

A solid ball lay just beneath the flesh now vacated by the baby and afterbirth. "That's the womb," she said. "It has to knot like a fist so the mother doesn't bleed too much. She's all good now." She patted Amanda's bloody thigh with one of her bloody hands. A momentary image of Priscilla observing this scene flashed before me. Somebody would be picking her off the floor or running to catch her—I couldn't decide which.

Instructed to wash the baby while Mrs. Foster finished with Amanda, I held him in my lap and gently applied a cloth Grandma Frances gave me along with a pan of tepid water and a caution about the soft spot at the top of his head. I'd never seen a newborn before, but from the fine dark hair smoothed from bathing to the tiny feet to the fingers that replicated closely those tending him, this one appeared flawless. Mrs. Foster took over for the diapering and belly wrapping. As I handed him off, bluish-gray eyes opened wide and appeared to look straight into mine. "It's as if he knows me," I said.

"Maybe he does," she replied. "He is a beauty, but then, he'd almost have to be."

We were on the road before the lightening of the sky. No moon that night appeared, just a dark blanket of pinpricks overhead. Back at the house, Mr. Foster met us, unhitched Millie, and led her to the barn.

"We'll talk in the morning," Mrs. Foster told me as I climbed the narrow stairs to bed. As tired as I was, her words circled in my head—as ineffective and odd as a butter churn without a paddle.

* * *

I awoke to early morning sounds—the shaking down of ashes in the kitchen range, the crowing of the red-crowned rooster, and the raucous warning of cicadas that harvest time waits for no one—familiar by then and at the same time insubstantial to one whose future remained up in the air. I washed in my basin and dressed in fresh clothes, finding the length of everything I owned shrinking. Somehow, I'd have to come up with a remedy for that.

Downstairs, Mrs. Foster was alone in her kitchen, rekindling the fire and centering a large griddle on the cooking surface. Milking and tending the animals had taken Mr. Foster outside, and summer allowed the girls a later wake-up. I perched on the edge of a chair, fearing I would burst if she didn't explain her cryptic comments soon.

"Do you remember Amanda from school or church?" she began, her volume dropping to a confidential level.

I cleared a nervous throat, but my voice still cracked. "Not really."

She adjusted the flue and took the chair across from me at the table. It wasn't the first time I felt her reading my mind, but courtesy required that she ask first. "Do you want this slow and easy or right to the point?"

"To the point, please."

"That baby boy we helped bring into the world last night is your half-brother, your father's son. And Amanda isn't the first girl he's messed with, but she and her grandmother, who can be a spitfire when it comes to her granddaughter, were the first to speak up and force the church leaders to do something." She took a breath and dropped her voice even lower.

"There are three other incidents that I know of involving your father. One resulted in a hurry-up wedding to a young man who worshiped the reverend and went along with the farce. The second girl came from people of means who sent her to an aunt in Pittsburgh. The aunt pretended the baby was hers. Imagine stuffing a bolster inside your bloomers and pretending it's a baby."

Mrs. Foster's attempt to insert levity into the situation failed. She noticed something going on with me that prompted her to hand me a cup of water and watch as I drained it. "The third one is the saddest. To spare her reputation, one girl used a knitting needle. . . ." She paused.

I realized I was shaking my head so violently that my hair tumbled out of the bun I'd pinned up minutes before. Yes, Papa had been unkind, even cruel to Mama, and he hadn't cared a fig about me. I'd learned to smile and say, "Thank you," when a church lady patted my hand and told me what a wonderful father I had. I hated my cowardice nearly as much as the fraudulent charm he put on display when people who mattered were present.

But this? Preying on girls little older than his daughter? Allowing others to pay for his sin? What was I to do with this unfathomable truth? The wounds from its jagged edges cut deeper than watching Mama's suffering, deeper than witnessing her death. I thought I'd faced the worst. This was too much to bear all at once—an overstuffed package stretched beyond capacity.

Before Mrs. Foster could grab me, I jumped to my feet and charged out the door. Full daylight had arrived, and Mr. Foster was carrying a large bucket filled with Hilda the Holstein's generosity. I ran past him, past the fenced garden with its loaded tomato stakes and succulent ears of sweet corn tasseled in silk. I circled the barnyard and tore across the sloped pasture all the way to Jennings Creek. My head was pounding, and my heart was ready to burst as I ran toward the water's edge. I slipped on the moss beneath a pine so old only its highest branches remained, fell to my side, and gave myself over to despair.

I don't know how long I lay there before I heard someone calling. "Belle! Where are you, Belle?"

It was Priscilla. I couldn't let her catch me like that. With cupped hands, I dipped water from the creek and scrubbed at my face. Then I stood combing fingers through my hair. What tale could I invent to explain my whereabouts?

She came into view and jogged down the slope. "Belle, what's happened to you? Mama's worried sick and sent me to find you."

The ring of sincerity in her voice urged another binge of tears. I swallowed. "Your mama told me what really happened with Papa. "

"Oh, dear—I thought so. She was afraid you'd hear things from people who don't care about your feelings." Priscilla took a comb from her pocket and began to untangle the mess I'd made of my hair. Her touch was soothing and so gentle. I again fought the urge to cry. When she finished, we headed back toward the house.

I realized I hadn't heard the last girl's fate. "What happened to the girl with the—"

Priscilla cut off my question. "She bled to death, but only three people in the whole world know the truth—Mama, Doc Barnes, and the girl's mother. Everybody else thinks her appendix burst."

I couldn't fathom the poor girl's desperation, but that too lay at my father's feet, just as the unhappy outcomes of every girl he'd misused, whether they'd been pregnant or not. It would take a long time to make peace with the harsh facts that had been laid out that morning. Mrs. Foster's approach in telling it all at once was her way of minimizing my pain—one stroke of the scalpel, even a big one, is easier to take than a dozen.

Priscilla and I had reached the edge of the meadow when I realized I couldn't let her illogical statement stand, any more than I could ignore her confusion of subjects and predicates. "Your mama and Doc and the girl's mother aren't the only ones who know it wasn't the girl's appendix," I said, noting her confused expression. I pointed to her, then to myself, and then raised all five fingers.

It took her a minute. Then she gave me what I called "the Priscilla look."

"You always have to be the smart one, don't you?" She huffed off ahead of me and was sitting on the porch swing, ignoring me when I reached the house.

Margaret banged through the screen door and threw her arms around my waist. "I thought you ran away! But you wouldn't, would you, Belle? Promise me you wouldn't!"

By then, we were in the kitchen where Mr. Foster sat at the table, nursing a cup of coffee, the perfect picture of a man who lives and labors among women. One by one, Mrs. Foster was turning the pancakes lined up like soldiers on her griddle. Anyone who didn't know her well might think she was annoyed that breakfast had been delayed.

An immense tome lay on the table at my place, its cover affirming years of hard use. I approached the book with reverence and read its title: *Gray's Anatomy*. Mrs. Foster turned from the griddle, spatula in hand.

"It's about time we had a midwife around here who can speak Doc's language. And give the old coot a run for his money."

Coal Towns

we dig into the belly of our mother
so that we can have light
by which to bring across
our right-eous values
to this next, not new, generation
to these crying distractions,
these should-haves

and for the flood lights that shine
on these tackle-trained
blue-eyed boys
while they learn to
be hard hitters
on fake-grass with lines
they are trained to cross

who burn diesel fuel on backroads
and believe that they are chosen
when they are only
illuminated
by the burning
carved-out fat
of their mothers

Two Coal Poems

I.
Don't come here, Mister Money Man.
I'd just as soon string you up,
provided I can find an ash tree
not already felled by profit bugs.

But you're not here at all, are you?
You might sit in a high-back chair
on Wall Street, Dowsing your Jones;
You might sit in a Lay-Z-Boy recliner
on Maple Drive, snacking blue chips;
You might just sit at the cash register
on Main Street, tugging the teat
of the American cash cow Dream.

You see that mountain over there?
Of course you don't, cause it's gone.
My grandpappy lived on that mountain.
They used to say he knew these hills
like the back of his hand, because his feet
had stepped on every square foot of this county.
Hunting.   Preaching.   Visiting.
Of course, them people's gone now, too.

Your company shaved that mountain bald,
then sucked the guts right out of it,
then flung the leftover flesh over the side
to rot the creeks for miles around.
After you raped it, you left it for dead.

Not to worry, their suit-n-ties crooned
when we went all mountain-man on them.
"We can reclaim the land."
Now it's a golf course used by their buddies
that sashay from the cities in shiny cars.

Not a single dead coal miner plays there,
that I know of.

II.
Clean coal technology, the money men warble.
It would save a few inhuman, unsafe jobs.
But why don't you ask my great-great-grandmother
who died a century ago, when mountain folk
could not afford fancy zinc or granite on their graves,
what she thinks about clean coal technology.
In her day, they used limestone:
Hard, plentiful, cheap.
After their grandparents scrabbled hard
to carve a grip on these backcountry ridges,
they thought they'd bought eternity.

But coal puts things in the air
that curdle the milk of the sky.
It's so pale, you can't even see it
in the rivulets that gully gravel roads
on Pine Mountain, Newman Ridge,
or the Allegheny razorbacks.
It moved so slow, no one noticed
for decades that the rain was erasing
the old tombstones. Chemical reactions
of limestone and acid rain gouge out
the face of the rock, blur words,
even completely remove them.

Eternity was.

Clean coal, meet clean limestone.

Now what's the next acid
you want me to swallow?

Linda Mills Woolsey

At the Ice Cream Stand in Saegertown

Butt ends of bullets stand in for stars
on black T-shirt's American flag as it waves
on his back, above a slogan's snarky threat.
Beside him, a skinny babe in tight jeans
slowly strokes her baby bump.

Ahead of her their runny nose kid rubs his
grimy eight-year-old hands over the shelf
where they'll slide out our orders. Aside
from staff, we're the only ones masked,
though the virus still skulks even here.

I try to ignore the glares we're getting
from the crowd who think we're the ones
bent on bringing death to the party. Despite
the slogan, tough T-shirt is good with his kids,
stoops to their level, grins as he banters

with them. At two, the smallest remains
all frowns. Pink cowgirl shirt is maybe four.
Her glitter jelly sandals sparkle. Her nose
wrinkles as his trigger finger smooths back
strayed curls from her trusting upturned face.

Sharon Fagan McDermott

Hawk

(As the 21ˢᵗ Century Begins)

Something Stirs

It's mottled. Fluttering. A billowing lace curtain with mud smears on it, draped across the concrete. No. It's a pile of last autumn's leaves, raked from a new spring garden, mounded vertically on the wide driveway between my apartment house and the university's apartment building next door. I'm almost home, walking up the ironically named South Atlantic Avenue in this landlocked city of Pittsburgh. I squint at my driveway. Try to make sense of the nonsensical. What *is* that? I'm unsettled. Worries whirlpool in the dirt off the curbs. I'm barely scraping by teaching poetry—my dream job—as a full-time lecturer at the local university, heading home from teaching a Reading Poetry class where we discussed Joy Harjo's use of totem animals, prose poetry, stories from the Muscogee (Creek) Nation in her fierce book *In Mad Love and War*. My own decades-long mad love affair has recently ended. I'm at war with myself. The Clash's lyrics, *Should I stay, or should I go?* loop in my mind. I want to flee back to my family on the East Coast. I want a do-over, a new life—what's left for me here in my adopted city? But I also long for roots. Stability. To stop moving around. The breeze picks up, and something on the whatever-it-is in my driveway ruffles upward all at once, white, ethereal. I startle. That's no pile of leaves! I walk up to it. Crouch down. My brain, always in theater of the absurd mode, suggests *Pterodactyl*. No. Oh, no! It's a raptor, splayed wide on his back. His wingtips touch either side of the driveway. Red-tailed hawk? Peregrine Falcon? Why has he fallen from the sky? I peer at his face, eyes shut tight. My heart beats wildly. The streets are empty, save for me and this wild creature. What should I do? How can I help?

Brick and Feather

Pittsburgh is a red-brick city circled daily by red-tailed hawks. Bricks and mortar build the neighborhoods here—row on row of brick homes constructed on impossibly steep slopes and around the three rivers. A city as solid as its building materials. Most people who grow up in Pittsburgh rarely leave Pittsburgh, except, perhaps, for a four-year college experience elsewhere. But it seems they always return home. Its gritty urbanity is surprisingly lush with trees and punctuated by huge parks full of woodland trails to traipse. Deer, possums, raccoons, and wild turkeys show up in our backyards. The brick homes along my street once housed high-powered industrialists of the Steel City era. In its former iteration, my apartment was an intact mansion with a maid's quarters and an ornate entryway. Over the decades, it was divided into three apartments. I lived on the bottom floor with its wooden pillars carved intricately with flowers and vines. The kitchen was tacked on in the 1970s, and you could feel yourself sliding forward to a more casual era when you entered it. The garden sprawled in the long backyard, and standing there, looking up, you'd see the circling raptors riding thermals in the sky.

How Falling Begins

It's now 2003, one year after the death of my beloved father and two years after the terrorist attack on, and fall of, the World Trade Center. My beloved son, Brian, who lived with me for a year out of college, is now pursuing his dream of being a photojournalist. As a single mother, that moment of saying goodbye—of watching Brian move into the larger world as a young man full of hopes and goals (and expensive cameras and lenses) to pursue an MFA in photojournalism at the University of Montana—is a bittersweet moment. As this is his time to soar, it seems fitting that he is heading toward "Big Sky" country. But for me, it is an ungrounding moment as well. Just a few years into this new century, and the accrual of losses fills me with vertigo. I am in a slow-motion free fall. I have not yet arrived at that seismic moment when I will come home to an eviction notice tacked to my door. This won't happen until six months after the day of the red-tailed hawk's unprecedented collapse in my driveway.

I lean in to study the languishing bird. Tears spring to my eyes. It is a magnificent raptor. I'm sure it is dead (I hope it's alive). I marvel at the spectacular breadth of its wings, the score of dark brown bands across them; its white chest marked with brown streaks; its reptilian talons, yellow and curled; and the incisive curve of its beak. Wild or not, I want to lift it into my arms and comfort it. Its eyes are shut tight. The breeze coaxes its feathers to flight, but to no avail. It is still. Too still.

About Sky

My New Jersey childhood was all about sky. Lying in the sand close to the swells of the Atlantic, I gaze up at a parade of cumulus clouds overhead, radiant white in the sun. They call out for translation. Is that a stegosaurus or a mountain range? A float in the Macy's Day Parade or a giant stuffed cat? It seems to me that everything holds meaning. As I grew, I learned to read the signs of a changing sky. Tail ends of hurricanes punctuated our summers with their glowering cumulonimbus. Those black thunderclouds would sweep up the whole Atlantic Ocean and drop it all at once upon our small suburban community. Sky brought dramatic weather, but come April, sky brought wispy cirrus threaded with endless birdsong. Robins, cardinals, finches, sparrows, chickadees, and wrens descended on us, their melodies spilling through newly opened windows, while crows and gulls shared the lower-end tonalities of chortles and caws. Alone with birds, I talked to them. Lying under our backyard apple tree, I asked quiet questions of the wrens and the robins whose red breasts stood out stark against white petals (which floated like their own field of clouds above me). The sparrows mostly darted away, but every so often a robin would remain and cock her head—just like my dog—at my whispers. With a world so full of wonders, I gave myself a job: pay attention and try to make sense of it all.

Help and Panic. Panic and Help.

As far as I can tell, the hawk is not breathing. I snap myself from my shock—*DO SOMETHING!*—I grab my phone. But—who to call? I dial the Pittsburgh Zoo. Someone picks up: "Hello? Pittsburgh Zoo." I begin to ramble—too fast, too loud:

"... a bird in my driveway—big—giant!—Oh God, he's so beautiful! The boys next door drive too fast—oh shit! They'll be home soon—might run him over. I don't know if he's alive. I just can't tell. He's on his back; he's..."

The man's voice on the other end of the line is gruff: "I can't understand you!" His bellow slices through my panic. I take a deep breath and slow down and try to explain the pile of feathers in my driveway.

"What do you want me to do? We're a Zoo, not a Wildlife Rehab."

"Don't hang up!" I yell. Tears spring to my eyes again. "Do you have the Rehab Center's phone number?"

He gives me their number. Hangs up. The bird remains a neutral symmetry on concrete—taupe, brown, white, pale yellow. I dial quickly.

This time, a younger male voice answers at the Wildlife Rehab Clinic. In the midst of describing my dilemma, he abruptly cuts me off:

"What does the bird look like?" Does it have spots on its chest?" (*Please hurry! He might be dying!*)

"Yes, yes, he has spots, splotches, streaks, whatever you want to call them. They're brown. No. His eyes are closed. I can't tell if he's breathing. Look, my neighbors will be home soon, and they drive fast up that driveway. I don't want them to hit him!"

And then, the young man horrifies me: he chuckles. And chuckles again.

Should I Stay or Should I Go?

Do I need to explain the appeal of flight? The effortless soar, the currency of air and its dependable drafts that can buoy you, hold you aloft, show you impossible vistas? The sweet swoop of a life where and when joy finds you, lifts you higher? The exhilaration of soaring above all the muck and roil and jostling below? You have heard for yourself the celebration of geese in their V-shaped journey, a call and response with their beloved old ponds. You've watched the sun gild lavender-edged clouds and imagined a sleek ascent toward a crescent moon. Do I need to show you Leonardo da Vinci's ornithopter, the flying machine born from his beautiful imagination way back in 1490? It was whimsical. Splendid with its aerial "bones" and dragon-esque wings.

But I'm old enough to know life is not always going to be a spiraling upward; there are whole swaths of time when life firmly grounds you. When there's no soar in the hollow of my bones. My beloved father, dead. My dream job, which does not pay a living wage. My beautiful apartment, which I'll soon have to vacate because I can't afford the rent. My love of two decades, gone. My son, grown now and living in Montana. And who falls gracefully? Who can divine if the ground will break their fall or simply break *them*? Why the hell am I still here in this city without seas, where magnificent birds can drop from the sky?

Sometimes the Meaning lies Beyond You

Earlier today in my Reading Poetry class, we read Joy Harjo's "Eagle Poem." It begins:

To pray you open your whole self
To sky, to earth, to sun, to moon
To one whole voice that is you.
And know there is more . . .

I want the hawk to rise up and soar in circles above my head. It does not belong to the concrete. It does not belong to the brick and mortar of this city. It does not belong to me or my gaze. It belongs to the air, to the red rudder of its tail, to the elegant architecture of its wings.

I hold the phone in my hand. The rehab guy on the line stops laughing and apologizes.

"You must think I'm nuts for laughing," he says.

"I just *really* want to help this bird," I say.

"I'm pretty sure you're looking at an adolescent hawk who's still perfecting his dive toward prey. They've gotta learn, too. No hawk is born knowing how to dive up to 120 miles an hour. They've got to learn when to pull up before smacking the ground. Trial and error. Sometimes they don't brake fast enough. They can hit hard. Knock themselves out. I'll bet you anything your bird is unconscious and will come to soon. Give him some space. If he doesn't wake up, call me back."

I gaze down at the still raptor one more time. The spell of his fanned-out feathers. His symmetry, color, and pattern. A creation that makes sense, though not yet the perfect predator. I gently stroke his wing feathers. And suddenly, there is discernible movement. He gives a small shudder like a sigh. I quick-step back up the lawn and watch in wonder as the hawk slowly opens his eyes: two pale yellow suns open and close and open again to the sky. Relief floods me. Slowly, the raptor gets to his feet. Shakily, he peers down at his talons inexplicably on concrete. He holds his wings fully out for a moment and then folds them in, each feather perfectly aligned. I hold my breath. He has not yet spotted me standing mere feet away. And when his keen eyes *do* pierce the air between us, and when he turns a laser focus on me for a long second, I feel x-rayed, seen to the bone. Something shifts in me. In the gold rays of his gaze, I feel inexplicably buoyed. Better about my life. Giddy enough to break into dance.

Then, some comic relief: the hawk staggers a few steps forward like one of the regulars at Howard's Pub. He gives his brown-feathered head a slow shake, emerges from his daze, and in a flash, opens the dazzle of his wings and lifts off. My heart rises with him. He lands atop the telephone pole across the street, where he regains his composure for another five minutes and surveys South Atlantic Avenue one more time. A beacon in the harbor. A light that fell to earth. I am tipsy with gratitude. Ready to move forward. I hold myself in a pool of late afternoon sun for as long as I can. He leans forward on the pole's precipice, then opens his magnificent wings and soars, disappearing into sky.

From Basketstar to Bipolar

after *Roget's Thesaurus of Phrases*

Without a doubt, with north compass surety, I know
       that someday you will be safe as a basket star, which is
neither basket nor star, but a sea creature protected
       from all vagaries of weather, regret, ambition. Here

the right to bear arms translates to sleeveless tops
       in April, sundresses in June by the aviary, where each
person is acutely aware that, flimsy as we may appear, each of us
       is a load bearing wall in the palace of the world. Here, beasts

of burden are recognized, packs lifted off their backs,
       soft bristled brushes pulled through their matted hair,
bags of oats placed near troughs of melting snow. Here
       the upper crust crumbles, their tortes topple. Here, those

who've slept on beds of nails, who've been imprisoned, who for years
       looked out of one small window, six inches of sky, for them
mile high observatories, telescopes, vast desert nights, for them,
drinks
       mixed with moonlight, floor shows featuring

binary stars stepping out. Here, valleys bombed by dictators
       fill with rain, turn to kettle lakes where on Sundays children
       race
sailboats. Here, all the facts that were beside the point, immaterial,
       gather at the courthouse steps, a class action, find their legs,
       cake walk

up those stairs wearing three-piece suits, performing without
objection,
  interruption, refusing to cease and desist, part of the public
domain, unsuppressed, justly, duly, finally. Noted. Here, those
who've found
  themselves between the devil and the deep blue sea,

suddenly find the waters parted. Here, those who were bipolar,
locked into
  roller coaster rides, bumper cars, ghost houses for months at
  a time,
get to take the train around the park, watch giraffes reach their tall
  necks, gather leaves around their wet, full lips.

I Named Him David

My couch eats me; or is it a sofa?
This poem is not about my brother.
Cement high-rise replaces Poli's Seafood
Restaurant; lobster door handle stays.

St. Rosalia's fish fry odor lingers.
Porch pumpkin's jack-o-lantern
smile wilts into a grimace.
Cold metal gurney, silver elevator.

Path pebbles half-sink into mud.
This poem is not about my brother.
Leather-soled shoes slip in the rain.

Windshield blades squeak across frost.
White flakes leap.

Did I eat today?

I Saw It. It Happened.
It Keeps Happening.

He belts Rob. Hard. I see. *Never lie!* Whip! Rob is five. He makes me see. Whip! He cries. My little brother screams. I can't help. Forced to watch. Wrack. Racked and wrought. Whip! He'd unbuckled his belt, slipped it through the loops, coiled it in his hand. Rob screams. I scream inside. My little brother, hurt. *Never lie!* A tiny fib Rob told. I can't help. I hate him. Rob in his cowboy hat, cowboy boots, sang *Home on the Range*, pistols drawn, Capitol Theater, kids' day. In bed that night Rob sings *My daddy died over the ocean, my daddy died over the sea.* Whip! I stare at the round table where Mother and I sit, forced to watch. Oak grains stare back, swirl outward, come together, never quite meet. Whip!

The Storm

it leaps out of the water
soars into the sky with a howl
and splits clouds with electric teeth
its great paws thud into the earth
it comes tumbling over the hills
and releases a flood from its thick coat
it spins and drips and drenches the trees
snapping them in half with its force
leaves and branches sputter into the wind
you can smell the wetness of its skin
and feel the ground coming alive
in its dance with the wild thing

The Best of Time

The town of Dogwood was a bunion on the hillside of two river valleys in the coal-filled hills of Northwestern Pennsylvania. A flood wall kept the town confined to a narrow kidney on the valley floor, forcing the town's uphill spread, where second-floor windows looked out on tombstones at the same level. Downtown was a bowl—a wet place that drained poorly after the first frost when the ground hardened. Within this bowl, among the clustered buildings where insulation stuck out from exterior panels like overstuffed toys, was a rectangular ring of cropped turf and yard lines.

As football pads clattered under the November sky, a cold wind came up through the valley and over the flood wall where it kicked up dead leaves and rattled the wooden fence surrounding the field. Mitchell's scalp prickled, but he kept his hood down as he watched a player in white and red tackle the fullback in burgundy somewhere between the five-yard line and the goal. Two coaches sauntered over from the sidelines and met near the goal. Before long, they came to a resolution, and the home team's offense dragged themselves back to the ten-yard line.

Mitchell stood on a crate, arms crossed over the creaking wooden fence, when a voice came from below. "Want one?"

He ignored it.

"Shit, sorry," his friend David said. David tapped Mitchell's leg to get his attention and held up a pack of Marlboros. David repeated, a few degrees louder, "Want one?"

Mitchell nodded. He took the pack, fingered out a cigarette and lighter, and lit up. When he handed back the pack, the older man was shaking three white tablets from a sandwich bag into his palm. He tossed them into his mouth and chewed. David had been handsome before— more filled out, with deep blue eyes. Now he was gaunt and pale. As he crushed the pills between his molars, the hairless patch of scarred tissue over his temple writhed and stretched like a worm burrowing through his skin.

Catching Mitchell's eye, David shrugged. "Migraine." His hands were shaking by the time he grabbed the pack. "What's the score?"

"Twenty-eight and two."

David spat, "Come on." The two men walked around the outer perimeter of the wooden fence. They cut through backyards with rusted-out American muscle cars covered in shabby blue tarps and then walked around half-standing chain-link fences until they reached the high school. The Boyd County school bus squatted vacant in the parking lot. Even the driver was catching the game.

David was mumbling something under his breath, but Mitchell paid him no mind. For a time, he had tried to parse what was being said, but he had long ago accepted that the former army ranger spoke of things known only to himself. Mitchell watched as David pulled out a six-inch Buck Knife from a belt sheath and stabbed at a tire. The point bounced and skidded down until it hit the metal rim.

"Goddammit," David grumbled, trying again, then again. Mitchell watched David in his stabbing fit for a moment before turning his gaze upward toward the ridge of the low mountains that appeared to him like the knobby spines of starving dogs. They hadn't welcomed him home. Mitchell's nail-less thumb traced the shiny white burned scar tissue on the tips of his fingers. An ache emerged between his shoulder blades where it found a nerve and rode down to his heel.

When David doubled in a coughing fit, Mitchell said, "Let's go."

David collected himself and guided them back around the field to his truck.

* * *

The ceiling fan in Micthell's room wobbled as it spun. It created a faint *whomp* he could no longer hear, but felt as the air beat across his arms. The blades were one part wooden veneer and two parts cobwebs that followed the blades like smoke trails.

From the living room, Mitchell heard the slapstick sound effects of Angry Beavers. It had taken a few weeks for his hearing to return, and while it hadn't recovered completely, he could make most things out. He hadn't told anyone else, but as his hearing returned, he played the part of someone still suffering from what they used to call 'hysterical deafness.' He had to explain himself less when people assumed he wasn't listening.

Still, he figured that his father wasn't watching the TV. The high volume was for the off-chance Mitchell's hearing was better than he'd let on. His father wasn't the type of man to let his son hear his weakness. Mitchell pictured the old man sitting in his recliner, shoulders slumped, sleeves wet with snot, tracing the corduroy upholstery with his fingers as he sulked into a cup of coffee, topping it off with something cheap and amber.

There was nothing Mitchell could do. Any attempt to tell his father he'd forgiven him would push the old man over the edge. It wasn't just sorrow in that chair, but self-loathing. His father sat beneath a wall covered in portraits of four generations of uniformed men—all looking down on him as the one who'd failed to raise a proper son.

Before Mitchell left for Iraq, his father had been outspoken about the duties of the modern American man and Mitchell's place. He believed the failures of the Homefront in the 70's had led to the rise in terror across the globe. He said it was up to Mitchell's generation to correct those errors.

Mitchell remembered when his dad had once picked him up from school and told him the people of Appalachia had been personally stabbed in the back during Vietnam. He said, "It was a goddamned shame. While my boys were bleeding out there, commie mine shirkers from here down to Kentucky were undermining their sacrifices with their strikes."

Mitchell knew that, for a while, his father had felt proud to have him as a son. He'd gone to every one of Mitchell's JROTC programs he could. When Mitchell paraded with the flag as a color guard, his father was always there, hand on his heart.

But after he returned from Iraq, his dad could hardly stand to be in the same room with him. Mitchell's hearing issues made things worse.

Instead of trying to have conversations at a higher volume, his father took to quick gestures and passive avoidance to deal with his own discomfort. That's why it was a surprise when his father opened the bedroom door and let in the sound of slapstick fighting from downstairs.

His father hadn't knocked. Mitchell kept up the deaf charade long enough that his father quit certain niceties.

As his father's bald head peeked into the room, he gazed at Mitchell for a moment before staring at something on the floor. His button nose and cheeks were shimmering red and oily in the nicotine-tinted ceiling light. His eyelids had been rubbed raw. He spoke in a whispery shout, like a visitor embarrassed to speak in a sick ward.

"Sergeant Major wants you in your BDUs for tomorrow."

Mitchell nodded. He stared over at a poster: Spiderman clinging to the glass wall of one of the Twin Towers.

"What about you?" Mitchell asked.

"Us older folks are going to be in service dress. He, um—he thinks you'll be an inspiration if the boys at the school see you in your cammies."

Mitchell eyed the green duffle bag tucked behind the bedroom door. Inside were the replacement BDUs he'd been issued, clean and starched, after his last pair had been shredded. His stomach curdled at the thought of wearing them again.

"Where's it going to be?"

"Downtown. The high school field."

* * *

The rain kept the ceremony indoors, pattering across the gym's rooftop in waves of deafening white noise. The floor's scuffed varnish reflected the dull burning orbs that passed for lights as they dangled from the ceiling in suspended cages. Bleachers stood as permanent fixtures of immovable wood, splinters, and mosaics of colorful wads of gum old enough to have tenure. Everything was covered in the school's official burgundy, from the bench seats to the championship banners that clung to the whitewashed brick walls and even to the strips of padding that walled both ends of the court.

The gym was crammed like a sardine can. The bench seats were filled with people standing on the stairs, in between the aisles, and shoulder to shoulder on the floor, where they tried not to step onto the court. Between the free throw line and midcourt, there stood four ranks of veterans in sundry uniforms. Aside from Mitchell and David, who wore camo BDUs, most had on dress uniforms. Dress blues stood beside older pinks and greens. The most prevalent were the Vietnam vets with their stiff collars. The most revered were the half a dozen who'd fought in Europe and the Pacific almost sixty years before. There were nearly thirty in all—from the sheriff and one of his deputies, to the postmaster, head surgeon, two firefighters, Mr. Wyndham, who worked at the IGA, and even Mitchell's father. Everyone in Dogwood had been raised by someone whose boots had been caked with the mud of foreign soil.

Where Mitchell stood, in the front row north of the division line, it seemed like the whole town was here. He knew that wasn't far off. Almost everyone in the county who didn't work at the hospital was currently trying to cram themselves into the gym for this Veterans Day commemoration.

This wasn't a random, freak turnout. It had been a hard year for the troops. Nearly a thousand dead in Iraq alone. People wanted another Memorial Day, and news of rekindling conflict in Fallujah compounded things. For three years, this ceremony had been a massive county-wide event. Mitchell felt a lump in his throat. This might be the biggest since the towers fell.

The crowd quieted at the entrance of the Sergeant Major, who took his place in front of Mitchell. The lean, Black man walked with a limp, and in the silence, Mitchell heard his damp soles squeak across the waxed court. When he snapped to attention, the others did too. Immediately, a pain in Mitchell's knees woke that he hadn't noticed before, along with a sharp ache in his shoulder blades as if someone was stabbing him in the back. If he kept his knees locked, he'd cut off the circulation and could faint, but when he relaxed, the pain from his shoulders zapped along the nerve, burning down to his right heel.

The color guard came first. They marched in well-oiled sync, and Mitchell recognized the boy carrying the Stars and Stripes. He'd been a sophomore in JROTC when Mitchell had graduated, but for the life of him, he couldn't remember the boy's name. He must be a senior now—ready to follow Mitchell down another bleary-eyed path. The boy, clean-shaven and with a look that betrayed pride, reminded Mitchell of himself from over a year ago, when he was the one carrying the burden of the colors across this very floor. The more he tried to focus on the boy's features, the blurrier they got. For a moment, he thought he saw his own awkward smile overtake the boy's.

When the color guard went to parade rest, a man came up from the crowd, a trumpet in one hand, a woman guiding him with the other. The woman, a nurse, Mitchell realized, guided the withered man to the free-throw line. He brought the trumpet to his lips and played a rendition of the "National Anthem," out of key and offbeat. As he played, the crowd gave a respectable, if uncomfortable, observance. Snickers and the cry of a small child were overwhelmed by the screech of the brass and the roar of the rain.

Mitchell stared ahead. Past the old man and up to the championship banners at the opposite wall which went back half a dozen decades, his eyes roamed. He tried to remember the last time he'd been in that gym. It must have been during graduation. After the ceremony on the field, many had wandered back inside to say goodbye to each other. He couldn't remember who he'd last shook hands with. Maybe Hinchcliff, who always said he wanted to be a Marine but never manned up to join. Jackson, with his cool smile, crooked nose, and ass pocket bulging with a can of Grizzly. Maybe it had been Gretchen, who, Mitchell had known, had harbored a secret crush on him since eighth grade.

It didn't matter. No doubt, they were all here now. No one ever leaves Dogwood unless it's through the recruiter's office. Everybody he'd graduated with was here—Jackson, Hinchcliff, Gretchen, and dozens of others who didn't come to mind—all of them looking down at him like a pitiful hero, an idiot who'd sacrificed his youth so they didn't have to. He forced his mind past them, past their stares and judgments as he felt their eyes on him, the latest in the line of heroic fools.

He forced his mind to drift back further. Already, the rain and the stares were falling to the wayside, but the discordant screech of the off-key trumpet kept bringing him back. The next time he remembered being in a gym had been on the eve of his deployment. It was early in the morning. He'd been on one of his brigade's first flights out. Everyone was bleary-eyed, some were crying. They'd spent the days before packing, and those with families remained together. Mitchell stood in the processing line, packs in his arms, while men around him kissed wives and hugged children. When the COs told everyone to hurry up, some went back for extra embraces.

The deployment ceremony that followed was a grueling slog. Once the out-processing and inventory checks were over, all the soldiers re-entered the gym in formation and stood at attention while friends and family sat on the bleachers and looked on with pained reverence. Mitchell remembered a baby crying as the brigade commander gave a pep talk that dragged on for over twenty minutes. He'd just wanted to be on the plane and in the air. The exciting part was almost there, and besides, everyone knew what they'd signed up for. No one married into the Army with the expectation that their soldier would stay home forever. Everyone had known for close to two months that this day was coming. No reason to drag it out; they should have been prepared. As he grew more frustrated, Mitchell began to stare at the back of a staff sergeant's head. The short man had a bug bite on the back of his skull that stared back at Mitchell.

They had left after that, but things got blurry from there. Suddenly, he's in south central Iraq, where his battalion is supposed to help watch a 25-kilometer stretch of road to ensure the supply line north remains uninterrupted. Disappointed—all the heavy fighting is farther north, up the Euphrates, and what's the point of being a kickass grunt with an M240 when there's no one to shoot at?—and frustrated because some jerk-off up the pipeline had mishandled the rotation between his battalion coming into the FOB and the ones who were supposed to be leaving, so he and about a dozen other fresh faces must bivouac under the desert sun for a couple days.

Things quickly fall into a sluggish tedium as dry as the sands. Every day, twice a day, Mitchell climbs into the gunner's seat on the back of a Humvee and—with fourteen others spread across three vehicles—patrols their route until they run into the ass-end of someone else's responsibility and they then turn around and head back. What begins as exciting excursions turns monotonous. The same scenery passes on either side: barren desert with the odd hut or small shack that rises out of the flatness like lone cuspids in a toothless mouth. Nothing changes on the horizon beyond the occasional herd of nomadic sheep or a midday mirage. It's the same route every day, twice a day, for weeks.

The men in his Humvee are always the same as well. Cpl. Menendez drives, Lt. Scowcroft works the radio and corrals the other two Humvees in the patrol while Pfc. Burbank and Spc. Charles ride in the backseat, and Mitchell works the .50 cal. Over a handful of weeks, he gets to know them. Menendez was a prior-service Marine before re-enlisting in the Army. He's short and tilts his head back like an old woman looking down her nose to see the road. Burbank enlisted because he lost a bet that Will Smith would win best actor in 2002. Charles can speak some Gullah. Scowcroft is simultaneously one of the smartest and dumbest men Mitchell has ever met. The lieutenant had managed to graduate college with a double major in physics and mathematics; yet, when he found out he was coming to Iraq, he'd started studying Pashto, only to discover the Pashtun don't live in Iraq, but Afghanistan. He keeps a little translation book tucked away in his blouse on the off chance he meets a Pashtun a thousand miles from home.

The sun's setting as they make the last trip back to base. It's their second round trip of the day, and Mitchell's Humvee leads the convoy back. There's a narrow stretch of road where a cluster of houses stands only a few meters away from the cracked asphalt. Engineers had checked it for IEDs three times today.

Mitchell is in the gunner's seat on the fourth pass when a buried mortar detonates. The ground around him turns to liquid and rises in a geyser of asphalt and dirt with a deafening swell as the world grows dark. He comes to on his back, staring at the sky as clouds billow overhead and the world calls back to him with a deafening silence. He looks down between his boots. He is lying in the dirt, having been thrown almost eleven meters, and there, just off the road, is the Humvee, upside down. It's billowing black smoke with the smell of burning rubber, oil, scorched marshmallows, and marzipan. He's panting but can't hear his own breathing, nor the whoosh of flames as they overtake the vehicle and follow the tracks of oil and diesel in glowing rivulets as the flammable liquid trickles down the outside of the metal box. His ears don't ring, but there's a pressure against his eardrums now, and everything is deafeningly quiet. He sits up and touches his ears, and his fingers come back red. He's so focused on his blood, he doesn't notice the puffs of dust kicking off the ground around him until the fifth one bursts close enough that he feels the vibration through the earth. Only then does he realize he's being shot at. He turns and sees a Humvee firing its M2 off to the west, bullets ripping through hovel walls like shattered pottery. He crawls on his belly towards the burning wreck to use it as cover as death zips soundlessly through the air around him. When he reaches the flipped truck, he sees what is inside, or rather, he understands what's happening but can't quite make it out as the glass is blackened with smoke and soot, but he knows that if he could hear, there'd be crackling flames, screams, and metallic banging as fists and boots pound the metal doors and glass of the upturned truck, while its outer walls steam and radiate waves of ocular heat in the desert air, and he knows that the melt resistant BDUs of the boys inside are dissolving.

"Mitchell?"

And then there's a hand pressed against the glass. Red streaks mix with black soot before the hand pulls away, only to return as a fist that pounds the window. Mitchell reaches out and grabs the door handle, feeling the heat of the truck through his glove. He sees the fingers of his glove are missing, his own fingertips are scorched and blackened, but the pain doesn't register, so he pulls at the handle, but it doesn't budge, and only then does he see that the door was deeply dented and jammed when it rolled.

"Son?"

And he doesn't know what to do, as he has no knife, and he looks around and finds no gun, so he rolls over and kicks the window, and every kick shoots pain from his heel and up his leg and into his back where it strikes between his shoulders. But the kicks don't break the glass or dislodge it from its frame, and Mitchell screams a silent scream, but knows it is deafening because he feels his jaw pop and his vocal cords shear and—

"Mitchell?"

He blinked. He was back in the gym, panting with tears wetting his cheeks. He looked down, and his hands were bleeding where, in clenched fists, his fingernails had cut crescent shapes into his palms. The room was quiet, save for the roaring rain, and his panting echoed throughout the space as everyone watched to see what he would do next. When the sergeant major reached out a comforting hand, Mitchell turned and ran out of the gym and into the downpour.

* * *

Days later, his dad knocked on the bedroom door for the first time in weeks. Mitchell had been too stunned by the sudden respect for privacy to respond, so his dad opened the door without an invitation. Again, the old man avoided eye contact, but this was different. He didn't seem embarrassed, just uncomfortable. He spoke quickly before closing the door, "They found David behind the IGA."

Mitchell watched the door close, but his gaze was rooted to the spot. His vision was useless as he tried to process what his father had just said. His mind was in neutral as his lizard brain pressed the gas, RPMs rising.

It was the migraines that had killed David. He thought about how his funeral would look. They'd say something about him being a badass, door-kicking ranger, but wouldn't mention how he'd come back from the Gulf War sick with something the doctors couldn't explain—something that gave him headaches which made him want to blow his brains out. How, when he returned, he could run eight miles in one go, but two years later, he'd be red in the face and wheezing after a single flight of stairs. They wouldn't talk about how he had shakes in the early morning so bad they would crack his teeth. Mitchell thought that at least he'd be buried high up on the hill, so he could look out over the valley—look down on everyone who did the same to the two of them.

* * *

The next day, Sergeant Major came. Mitchell was in bed, fidgeting with an old Discman whose cords had to be torqued a certain way for Layne Staley to scream through the headphones. Someone knocked on the front door during one of the auditory breakups. When he heard the NCO's voice rasp from downstairs, he wanted to crawl out the bedroom window and run. He didn't want to feel more shame, nor did he want the older man to come in and try to comfort him, to offer some fake pity when Mitchell knew the man harbored just as much disappointment as Mitchell loathed himself.

But it wasn't Sergeant Major who came to the bedroom door. The knocking was softer, and when Mitchell said, "Yeah?" The voice that responded was youthful. Mitchell felt panicked, but before he could tell the stranger to leave, the handle turned.

The kid from the color guard had acne scars across his chin and a slight drift to his eye which made Mitchell wonder if the boy would need a waiver to enlist. He was young and stocky, and looked around awkwardly. *Perfect for the recruiters,* Mitchell thought. As he opened the door, he gave an uncomfortable little wave to Mitchell who was sitting up, gripping the Discman.

"Your dad told me to just walk in. He said you wouldn't have heard the knock, but it felt weird. I don't know if you heard me. Sorry." In his embarrassment, the boy spoke softer than he intended. Instead of keeping up the charade, Mitchell nodded. He motioned to an old plastic chair in one corner in front of a box TV and a PlayStation.

The boy pulled the seat over and fidgeted with a shopping bag in his hand. "You probably don't remember me, but—"

"I do. Just not your name. Sorry."

The boy relaxed. "Ben Gordon. I was a sophomore when you graduated."

Mitchell nodded. "Still on the team?"

"Yeah. Fullback. And still in ROTC."

Mitchell winced. The kid was going to be a mirror to him. Some fool looking for macho fulfillment to get a pat on the back from some other fool who'd made the same bad decision decades prior. "I saw you in the gym. What do you want?"

"I just wanted to say that, um, well, to give you this." He passed the bag to Mitchell. "I think it could help."

He took the bag and pulled out a composition notebook and pen. As he fingered through the blank pages, his jaw tingled and he grew nauseous. "Did Sergeant Major send you?"

"No. It was my idea. I didn't know where you lived, so he drove me here."

"Why?"

Ben shrugged, "I heard what happened. I'm sorry. You probably get that a lot, but, um, my dad dealt with something similar."

"So, you think your dad's crazy like me?"

Ben pressed his lips tightly together and looked at the door like he wanted to leave. Then he turned back to face Mitchell. "He wasn't crazy. Neither are you. He needed help, and maybe you do too, but maybe it's not something someone else can give, you know?"

"You sound like a shrink."

Ben smiled. "I guess it wouldn't surprise you to hear that I want to study that in school—college, I mean, and commission after. Maybe then I'd be a bigger help, talking to people, you know?"

Mitchell forced back a scowl as contempt welled up. He watched the boy sit, fumble with the notebook, and try his best not to make eye contact. He wanted to grab the fool by the collar and scream in his face about all the good that'd do. About how fucking pointless it all was. About the nerve of this kid, to tell him what will and won't help when he hadn't seen shit.

Instead, he only said, "Noble."

"Listen. You don't have to do me a favor. No one's going to read what you write. You can burn it later for all I care. But I've heard getting it out helps." Ben looked around as if trying to find the right words. They never came. Instead, he stood, gave a quick, "I hope it helps," and "Goodbye," then left.

Mitchell looked at the journal in his hands and wanted to chuck it out the window. Why not? He pictured it in the rainy yard, a bloated corpse with swollen pages. The ink would run out from the bundle of paper like a weeping, abandoned thing. No. He'd keep everything inside and hidden away, for no one else, not even the notebook—only himself.

He laid back down and watched the fan twirl as the TV downstairs talked about John Kerry's loss and celebrated the 257th birthday of the Pennsylvania National Guard. He thought about David and the gym, about all the people he knew in town who probably felt ashamed and embarrassed every time they saw him. How he should do them all a favor and follow the path David had trod. He thought about how he didn't know any Gullah and wondered if any Pashtun were wandering around Iraq thousands of miles from home like he had been. He tried not to think about the Humvee, so he thought about a fullback in a know-nothing town that he hoped would one day keep someone like Mitchell from becoming someone like David.

He swapped the CD and wrapped the headphone cable around the Discman until he caught the static feedback of music. As Scott Weiland sang about being dead and bloated, Mitchell clicked the pen and wrote:

Before I left for basic, my father told me 9/11 was the best thing to happen to this country. He had never seen America so unified. He'd never felt so proud. He said that I was lucky to be living in the best of times.

He stared at the text. His reality was made permanent by the black ink bleeding through thin pages. He continued:

The town of Dogwood was a bunion on the hillside at a confluence of two river valleys in the coal-filled hills of Northwestern Pennsylvania . . .

Bandage

The boy's eyes dig through his father's garden
as he wanders between the bushes.
He intrudes as an invasive species.
His curious hands comb the unkempt hedges.

He blushes at the juice of a ripe strawberry.
His fingertips survey the hot-colored roses.
His palm bites the thorn, soft skin unthreads
and unspools blood nectar against the stems.

Before the boy can wake to the wound,
or his father from his Sunday rest,
his mother sees him and treats him
as all mothers do.

She brings the palm of his hand to her lips,
shades the stain of his cut with a kiss,
settles the wellspring from the boy's eyes,
and bandages the wound.

Early Spring

A clearcut
hillside, snow
covers all sins—

daffodils sprout
through a sofa's
rusted springs.

Echoes of Home

What makes northern Appalachia feel different? What gives it its real voice? With my hands hovering over the keyboard, the answer came quietly to me, but with certainty: memory. What's more real than memory?

That's how this essay began—not with a plan, but with a moment. The kind of memory that doesn't ask permission to show up. I call it my first real one. Not because it was the first thing that happened to me, but because it's the earliest memory I can follow from start to finish. It didn't come from a photo someone showed me or a story I heard growing up. It's mine. Everything before it—some flashes of a swing set, maybe a birthday cake, the vague idea that we had a dog—feels blurry and secondhand, like I'm watching someone else's recollections through a fogged-up window. This one feels different. It's grounded. It has weight.

I remember waking up confused. The room was dim—maybe it was still early, or maybe the hallway light was on. Something felt off even before I knew why. My dad was there, sitting beside me on the bed. He wrapped his arms around me before I could ask what was wrong. I hugged him back, still half-asleep, still not fully in my body. His voice was low and tight, like he was holding something back. He told me my grandmother had died. That was it. Just those words. I didn't understand them—not fully—but I felt the shift. I felt the grief in his chest as he held me. He was crying, or doing his best not to, but it still came through in small, shaking breaths. I didn't know what death really meant, but I cried with him anyway. That was enough to understand that something had changed.

The rest of that day is gone. Nothing before, nothing after. Just that stillness—just the two of us trying to understand something too large for words. That memory feels like the first real one. Maybe it's because that was when the world stopped feeling simple. Maybe, because it arrived so clearly, I started to cling to the ones that came after. Even if I didn't realize it then, some part of me began to understand that memory doesn't always stay—not unless you learn how to hold it.

The next set of memories comes slower. Everything blurs again until I think of my grandfather—my dad's father. His presence doesn't arrive in a flash; it builds gradually, like warmth creeping back into cold hands. I remember mowing the yard with him, riding along on his big orange Kubota tractor. That machine felt twice my size and still somehow the perfect fit for both of us. I'd fall asleep leaning against him, tucked under his arm, the steady hum of the engine and the gentle rise and fall of the land rocking me into quiet. The world moved beneath us, but he didn't. He was constant. I felt safe there—happy in a way I didn't yet know could fade.

He was warm, kind in a way that feels rare now. Steady in ways other people only pretend to be. Even as a kid, I knew there wasn't anything he wouldn't do for me. Nothing could've stopped him from chasing another smile out of me. After my grandmother died, he lived alone. We tried to ease that weight by visiting often—staying overnight, pulling out the blow-up mattress in the living room, and watching the same Scooby-Doo episodes until we could quote them by heart. I'd recite Shaggy's parts, and he'd fumble through Scooby's voice, laughing when he nailed the growl just right.

His house sat on a good stretch of land. A garage off to the side, trees crawling up the hill behind the backyard. We'd walk the property together, moving slowly, checking on the garden, tapping watermelons, measuring out squash, and getting frustrated together when the deer outsmarted whatever trick we'd tried that week to keep them out. Every bite out of a pepper felt like a personal insult.

He grew peppers, tomatoes, zucchini, lettuce—sometimes berries. Each season he rotated crops, testing something new. He'd harvest everything, rinse it under the spigot, and start chopping. No recipe—just habit. He loved zucchini and squash especially and made salads from whatever he'd pulled from the garden. It was quiet work, but never lonely.

Sometimes we wandered into the woods, listening to leaves crunch underfoot, carrying walking sticks or scouting for new ones. We'd stop by his sister's house—she had well water that, to this day, I swear tasted better than his. He taught me how to hunt without making it feel like a lesson, how to build a fire, how to watch a place closely enough to notice what had changed. Most of what I learned came from those woods or evenings in the garage—lessons I didn't realize I'd absorbed until years later.

They say the music you hear as a kid shapes your taste for life. I believe it. When I think of my pappy, I don't just remember what we did—I hear it. There's a soundtrack under those memories: AC/DC, "Great Balls of Fire," all kinds of rock and metal drifting from the radio in the corner of his garage. That radio had been playing for decades and somehow kept going long after it should've quit. Those memories don't work in silence.

That garage was where I learned what organization looked like. He had a large, open space filled with old bikes and machines—an old Chevy '85 Monte Carlo and a few Harleys in one corner—yet everything had its place. His toolboxes were packed, labeled, and consistent. Every drawer had a purpose. Every shelf was intentional. He's still the only person I've known who could say, "Hand me the 9mm socket," and go straight to it.

I helped him clean up after projects, putting tools back where they belonged after turning something simple—like a rubber mallet and a dented plant pot—into a spaceship. Along his gravel driveway, I learned how to ride a bike. That's also where I learned how to fall. I learned how to stand back up, rinse grit from a scrape with something brown in a bottle that stung worse than the fall itself. Sometimes I still feel those phantom pains. That same yard is where I learned to ride a dirt bike. It wasn't fast, but it had an engine, and that was all I needed to believe it was a Harley.

One ride stands out, mostly because it still gets argued about. I was riding along, confident and free, when a rabbit hopped beside me. In my mind, it challenged me to a race. I accepted. I was winning—until I wasn't. My eyes followed the rabbit, and I lost control. The handlebars slipped toward the creek, and the crash came fast. I remember being lifted out of the water, soaked and stunned. My helmet was already off, and my pappy's hands were checking me over—calm and focused. Later, I heard he'd beaten both my dad and uncle—young, fast coal miners—to the creek. No one questions that part.

The disagreement is what I was chasing. I remember a rabbit. They insist it was a car. Either way, I ended up in the creek, and that story has never left us. It gets told at every gathering, retold with laughter. The details shift, but the story remains.

After the garage and the creek, the next memories lead to Hampton, Virginia, where I lived with my maternal grandparents for just over five years. Both were born and raised in West Virginia. They went to high school there, met there, and didn't leave until later in life. They've lived in Virginia ever since—but they never stopped sounding like home.

Living with them meant new routines and steady changes. Still, there was comfort in the familiar: that Appalachian accent I already knew. It shaped my own. Mornings and evenings were filled with voices that sounded like where I was from, but at school, I was surrounded by kids who didn't know there was a West Virginia. My speech became a blend. Some differences stood out—"creek" became "crick," and "soda" was always "pop." Others were more subtle: the rhythm of speech, the soft drop of a syllable.

I once asked my grandmother why people said "pop." That question turned into a whole lesson. She explained how language changes across states, counties, even families. She talked about accents, borrowed words, and regional slang. I must've asked her a hundred more questions. I didn't know it then, but I was learning to hear culture.

She cooked from a little spiral-bound recipe book passed down from her mother. It was warped and taped together, but it held everything that mattered. Her fudge was famous—so sweet it made your teeth ache. She said the secret wasn't the ingredients, but the feel of the spoon. She'd cook and talk, telling stories about sleet-covered track meets or how she used to help my grandfather with English assignments. That always amused her—he liked math and hated writing.

I was the oldest of the grandchildren, which meant I saw the family table grow. During my years there, the dining room stretched steadily—new leaves added, chairs borrowed, kids squeezed in. My grandmother adjusted without missing a beat. She cooked for four, then six, then eight or more. Somehow, she always knew who liked what. I couldn't remember if I liked green peppers. She did. And even though she'd cycle through names before landing on yours—"Brandon, no, Bill, no—Mayson"—she never forgot who you were.

My grandfather worked—and still works—for the Newport News Shipyard. His job isn't one that gets much attention, but it's the kind that helps the world run behind the scenes. He played his part building the massive ships that carry the U.S. military across the ocean. Quiet work, demanding work, but proud work. At home, he liked to joke around—always throwing out one-liners and seeing who would crack first. Still, he came alive most outdoors, especially during hunting season.

Behind his house in pens he built himself, he kept over a dozen hunting dogs. That alone was rare for the area. We'd run them several times a month, even outside of season just to keep them in rhythm. Each dog had its own quirks, its own name, and its own place in the pack. My grandfather taught me how to stay silent when the dogs were tracking; how to move through brush without giving myself away; how to call them back when the day was done. He treated them like teammates—respected and trained, not pampered.

Some of my clearest memories from those years come from those hunts. I learned how to shoot both a shotgun and a rifle during deer season—long, quiet mornings spent in a blind or pressed against a tree, watching shadows move across the far edge of a clearing. As a kid, I'd often drift off, lulled by stillness, waking only when my grandfather nudged me gently to point out a deer in the distance. He never minded my naps. "That's what patience looks like," he'd say with a grin.

Rabbit hunting offered a completely different rhythm. It was quick, loud, and filled with bursts of motion—less waiting and more reacting. We'd release the dogs and listen closely, tracking the rise and shift in their barking as they picked up a scent. When the barking sharpened, the chase had begun. The goal wasn't just to follow—it was to predict. Rabbits always doubled back, so we needed to figure out where they would turn. I had to move quickly, read the path, and shoot with steady hands and quick judgment. Those mornings taught me how to walk for hours without tiring and how to use my ears more than my eyes. They taught me how to listen for the woods themselves.

One day left a deeper mark than the rest. We were following the dogs through the brush, and I must have been too focused on the chase. I walked right over a snake—possibly even stepped on it—without noticing. My grandfather stopped short behind me and pointed it out. It wasn't large, and it wasn't venomous, but realizing how close I'd come to it unsettled me in a way I still remember. The silence of it, the ease with which it had gone unnoticed, made my skin crawl. My grandfather remained calm, treating the situation as if it were just another part of the day. Maybe it was for him. For me, the rest of that hunt passed in paranoia. I watched the ground and the trees with equal attention, scanning shadows, half-convinced the forest was watching back. Even now, snakes make me uneasy. There's something about the way they move—so fast, so fluid, and with no warning—that still lingers in my spine.

Those hunts weren't just about the chase or the shots fired. They were about process. I learned how to clean game properly, how to skin without waste, and how to make jerky that tasted better than anything from a store shelf. My grandfather always said the reason it tasted better was simple: we earned it. Looking back, I think he was right. There's a quiet satisfaction in doing something start to finish, in knowing every step from the field to the plate. The pride wasn't in the kill—it was in the care.

That idea—of carrying something through—feels familiar. It's the way so much of life works in the region I come from. Individually, the things I've described aren't unique. Plenty of people hunt. Plenty grow gardens or cook from memory. What makes this region feel different is how all of it exists together, layered and lived in. Gardens sit beside gravel roads. Tools are passed down alongside stories. Families expand, and so do dinner tables. These aren't loud things. They're quiet, consistent, and embedded in the rhythm of daily life.

While working on this piece, those thoughts stayed with me. I didn't write it all in one sitting. The memories arrived slowly, sometimes when I wasn't trying to remember at all—while driving to work, standing in the shower, or halfway through making dinner. I'd follow a fragment until it turned into something whole, then decide whether it fit. When I finally sat down to reread the full draft, it struck me that none of it felt as complete as the memories themselves. Somehow, writing them down made them smaller. They felt reduced—still accurate, but not quite enough.

Memory rarely arrives in full. Scientific studies even suggest that each time we remember something, we alter it slightly. What we recall becomes a version revised with each telling. Even knowing that, I still believe these moments carry weight—not because they are perfect records, but because they remain. I can still hear boots in leaves, taste rain in the air, and feel the hum of an old dirt bike. These memories aren't static. They've been carried.

This kind of writing isn't where I typically feel most at home. Most of what I've written in the past leaned toward academic structures—assignments, responses, answers to someone else's question. Fiction, especially fantasy, has always been more comfortable. I've always enjoyed building something imagined, something that didn't exist until I wrote it. What surprised me is that this essay followed that instinct. Each memory found a shape, and the whole thing started to read like a narrative. The structure of storytelling crept in, even when I didn't plan for it.

That process gave the work its own rhythm. It helped me move between what I chose to include and everything I left unsaid. So many memories remain unwritten—but choosing between them made space for reflection. The ones I left out still shaped the ones I kept, and even now, they sit just beneath the surface, part of the pattern.

That brought me back to the question that had been sitting beneath the surface since I began: what makes northern Appalachia feel different? What gives it its voice?

Is it memory? I'm no longer certain there's one answer. I don't think there ever could be. It's not a single story or a checklist of traits. The identity of this place is built from the ground up—through repetition, through inheritance, through small acts carried out again and again until they become second nature. It's the way families gather, the way tools are used and put back in place, the way food is prepared more from memory than from instructions. These are habits passed down without ceremony, patterns you don't realize you've learned until you catch yourself repeating them.

Writing this made those layers rise to the surface. I found myself remembering the quiet moments more than the loud ones—the way gravel feels beneath your shoes after a storm, or the exact pitch of a laugh heard across the yard. I started to recognize just how much I'd carried with me. Even now, I feel the weight of it—not heavy, but constant.

Nothing I've written here is meant to define Appalachia, and certainly not northern Appalachia on its own. No single voice can. What I can offer is this: the memories that shaped me, the rhythms I grew up with, and the small truths I've learned to keep. These pieces—the garden rows, the gravel roads, the smell of rain in the air—may not sound like much on their own, but when lived in together, they begin to hum. They form a kind of music only familiar to those who've grown up in it. It's a low, steady sound—like a tractor idling, a dog's bark carrying across a hollow, or the last log crackling in the wood stove as the room dims.

Even the town I'm from tells part of that story. It has a single stoplight. That's what we tell people when they ask where we're from. It's the detail that sticks. A friend of mine once said the only interesting thing about his hometown was that it was named after George Washington's brother. Maybe that's true. For me, the most interesting thing about mine is that it doesn't need anything flashy. It just is. It exists in memory, in motion, in return.

There's comfort in that. Appalachia isn't always loud, and it doesn't always demand attention. Often, it sits quietly, waiting for you to notice the things that don't get written down. The back porch chairs that never move. The way your grandmother cycles through everyone's name before landing on yours. The moment you realize that even when you forget whether you like green peppers, she still remembers. These are small things—but they are kept.

If writing this piece has taught me anything, it's that memory doesn't have to be complete to be true. It doesn't need to be perfect or exact. What matters is that it's carried forward, that it finds its way back into your hands when you need it most. That's where I think the voice of this region lives—not in the declarations, but in the returns.

The Altoona Curve

twilight breaks, screams from the descending
Skyliner, the smell of candied almonds
on the concourse, a stand of Eastern White Pines
near a ridgetop, the slow chug
of a Norfolk Southern engine climbing, cool,
thick, damp summer night air, a girl
orders a Boston shake at Burger Hut
as a tuner in a rusted-out Integra races past
down Buckhorn Road, a newborn sleeps
in a room with open windows, the curtains
sway drowsily, a meadow of lightning bugs,
a Sheetz clerk takes a smoke break near
the kerosene pump, the shortstop for the
Akron Rubberducks strikes out
to end the game. Fireworks.

Arlene Weiner

Mint Chocolate Chip

Lenny doesn't live in town,
but his girlfriend does,
and he stays with her a lot.

Last night he went into her kitchen
and dished out mint chocolate chip ice cream
for the four of us. It was delicious.

He buys it from a woman who
brings it back from Penn State
where you can major in ice cream.

Sometimes she has one flavor,
sometimes another. Bootleg ice cream.
Lenny knows his way around.

The Creek Already Knew

Cheat Lake isn't a real lake. It's a dammed river with too much confidence—wide and murky, shaped like someone forgot to finish drawing it. The banks are steep in a way that feels intentional, like the land is keeping its distance from the water. People fish there. They take family portraits in coordinated flannel. On weekends, couples paddle around in rented kayaks like they're trying to save their marriages. I go to the edge sometimes just to sit. Not because it's beautiful—which it is—but because it's quiet, and the wind moves like breath there.

We moved to Cheat Lake in December, the month I turned thirteen. Dad got promoted to regional operations director for Truform Plastics, and Mom called it a blessing. I believed her. She said it like she meant it, not like someone trying to convince herself. I like that about her—she never fakes the big things. She lines our shelves with great books. She smears oil pastels onto canvas by heart.

Dad likes numbers. Not math, but *numbers*—the way they behave. He's good at systems, order. I think I got that from him—the love of control. Which is funny, since the only reason I'm alive is because my heart didn't form the way it was supposed to—a bicuspid aortic valve, a simple surgery when I was six, followed by a lifetime of "monitoring."

I want to be a pediatric cardiologist. Not because of what happened to me—I hate when people make that assumption—but because I like knowing exactly what's broken and exactly how to fix it. Also, because I think the heart is the most dramatic organ. It behaves as though it feels things. I get that.

My name's Simon. I wear boat shoes and I condition them when they dry. I write poetry in a leather notebook I ordered online and hide in my nightstand; not rhyming poetry—nothing about "the moon" or "your smile," but more like "the way a boy looks away from you a second before you look at him."

I love T.S. Eliot, and I recently discovered slam poetry on YouTube. There's one video I watch at least once a week. It's called "I want to buy a sloth with you." The poet wants to love someone by loving something slow—something un-leaveable. It's stupid and brilliant and weirdly romantic, and when I watch it, I feel like something inside me is trying to reach through the screen and touch the speaker's voice.

I haven't told anyone about the poem. Or the notebook. Or the fact that in gym class, the boys in my grade are loose and loud. They smack each other's backpacks while walking down the hallway and call it friendship. They talk about girls like they're competing in a game I don't understand. Two of them—Tucker and Bryce—have visible abs. I know this because in gym they wipe their faces with the bottoms of their shirts, lifting the fabric deliberately, like they're performing a magic trick. They glance sideways afterward to see who noticed. Everyone noticed.

After school, I walk to the woods across from our subdivision. My little brother Charlie follows sometimes, and sometimes, we run into Cade and his friends—neighborhood boys who act like they invented the forest. They call it "the trails," but it's just deer paths and old logging roads, overgrown and full of smashed soda cans. There's a lean-to made of sticks and plywood that we pretend is a fort. Cade keeps a pack of gum hidden under a rock near the creek. He says it's the "supply stash." I think he likes the idea of surviving something.

Cade is magnetic—not in the fake way people say it to mean "cool." I mean he pulls. Your eyes. Your attention. The air in your lungs. He has a chipped tooth and permanent grass stains on his jeans, and he always walks like he's late to somewhere better. He's thirteen, like me, but talks like someone who's already kissed three girls and not told anyone about it. I don't think I want to kiss him, exactly. But sometimes I imagine what it would feel like to sit very close to him without either of us moving away.

I told him once that I write poetry. I didn't mean to. We were sitting on a log watching the creek drag sticks around the bend like toys on leashes, and he asked what I did after school. And I said, "Sometimes I write poems."

He just nodded. "Like love poems?"

"No." I said it too fast.

He smiled without looking at me. "My mom writes songs. She calls them 'poems with purpose.'"

I wrote that line down later: poems with purpose. I liked the way it sounded. It made me wonder if any of mine had one.

At school, I keep to myself. Mrs. Hanson calls me "introspective" and says I have an "old soul," which, I think, is her way of explaining why I don't talk during group work. Most kids in my grade orbit each other with nervous laughter and inside jokes about YouTubers I don't watch. I pretend to check my phone a lot, but I'm just staring at the home screen. It's safer to look preoccupied than curious.

But in the woods, it's different. I can study things without being seen—the way Cade throws rocks underhand, always with his left hand; the way Charlie tries to keep up but stays two steps back; the way the creek hums when it's low and sings when it's full; the way Cade once slipped, caught himself on my arm and didn't let go right away.

I think the creek knows—about me—about all of it.

The winter after my fourteenth birthday, I went to the Valentine's dance. Not because I wanted to (I didn't), but because I was invited, and saying no felt like the kind of decision you remember twenty years later with a wince.

My date was named Chelsea, and she sat across from me in art class. She wore mismatched earrings on purpose and once sculpted a ceramic bear wearing an "Occupy Wall Street" hat and labeled the sculpture "Performance Piece." I liked her because she said exactly what she meant, and because she drew people with five fingers on each hand, which made her more technically gifted than anyone else in the room.

She asked me if I wanted to go "ironically," and I agreed. I didn't really know what that meant. I still don't.

We went with a group, five of us in total, all from the "back table" in art. The girls wore boots and glitter eyeliner, and one of the boys wore his dad's tie and a belt with cartoon bacon on it. I wore a navy v-neck sweater over my most structured button-down. My mom tried to slick my hair into something called a "gentle swoop," which made me look like a very tense news anchor.

We took pictures in Chelsea's driveway. Someone's mom handed out sparkling grape juice and said, "This is just the cutest," which made me want to dissolve into the gravel.

The dance was in the middle school gym, which had been tragically over-committed to a "Paris Under the Stars" theme. There were string lights, a paper Eiffel Tower, and a suspicious amount of artificial fog. Someone had hung a banner that read "L'amour est magique," which I'm pretty sure was copy-pasted from Google Translate and glitter-glued with chaotic confidence.

When we walked in, "Buy U a Drank" was playing at a decibel level that felt physically inappropriate. It vibrated in my chest like a second heart.

Chelsea started dancing immediately. I stood nearby and pretended to drink my Dr Pepper like it was a serious commitment. Cade was there too—in jeans, a Henley, and the same impossible ease he always wore like good cologne. He was standing by the bleachers with his friends, watching the crowd with a smirk like none of this had the power to touch him.

He saw me. He nodded. I nodded back.

I had no idea what either of us meant by that.

"Dance with me," Chelsea said, pulling at my wrist.

"I don't know how," I lied.

"That's fine," she said. "You can be bad. It's democratic."

I almost laughed. She meant well, but I had gone to a school in Kentucky that was thirty percent Black, where middle school dances were not about democracy. They were about survival. Dancing wasn't an equalizer. It was a stratifier, a map of who had rhythm, who had social capital, and who, by eighth grade, had already learned to pop-lock like they had a future in it.

I thought of Rousseau just then. "The origin of inequality is in the first man who fenced off land and said, 'This is mine.'" Had we grown up together, I think he'd have added, "And then did the Soulja Boy on it, perfectly, while the gym clapped along."

So, yes. I could dance. I had learned early—quietly, diligently—because it was safer to surprise people with grace than to be dismissed outright.

I let the beat settle into my chest, timed the drop, then let go—not completely, not foolishly—but with precision. Controlled hips, confident shoulders. Enough irony to seem aware, enough sincerity to make it count.

Chelsea's eyes widened. "Holy shit, Simon."

I shouted. "I contain multitudes."

We danced hard through three songs. Her eyeliner smeared from sweat. My collar stuck to my neck. At one point, we did a synchronized shoulder pop that got actual cheers. She grinned like she'd just discovered fire.

I didn't stop watching Cade. Not entirely. He was leaning against the bleachers, pretending not to see me. But he saw. I knew he saw.

He always saw things when he thought no one was watching.

Then "Bleeding Love" came on, and everything shifted.

Not because of the song, but because it was the first slow one, and suddenly people were pairing off like some kind of social emergency drill. Chelsea looked at me. "Should we?"

I swallowed. "Sure."

We did the middle-school sway—arms awkwardly placed, our bodies separated by enough air to house a raccoon. Her palms were warm, and her eyes were kind. She looked over my shoulder and whispered, "This is so deeply weird," and I laughed.

Over her shoulder, I saw Cade dancing with a girl in a red dress. He had one hand on her waist and one at the base of her neck. He leaned in close and said something that made her laugh. His eyes flicked up toward me just for a second. Then back to her.

I looked away.

Chelsea leaned close and shouted in my ear so I could hear her over the music. "You okay?"

"Yeah."

"You're making that face," she said. "Like when Mr. Larkin gives us the division problems with all the remainders."

"I'm just warm," I lied again.

Suddenly, Chelsea stopped swaying. "We don't have to do this if you don't want to. My cousin says dances are dumb anyway—basically just for standing around and pretending to have fun."

I almost laughed, but the sound got stuck. She watched the lights flick across the floor. "If you like someone else—I don't care. I'm not gonna freak out."

I stared at her. Words wouldn't come.

She smiled. "My mom says nobody marries their first dance partner anyway."

Across the gym, Cade's head tilted back in a laugh. I wondered if she saw the way my eyes went to him like a reflex, how I watched him like he was a planet that might hit the earth.

I couldn't speak. My mouth was made of stone. Or maybe jelly.

She squeezed my hand cautiously, like she wasn't sure if she should. "It's okay," she said. "You can like who you like even if it seems impossible. Nobody gets to pick that."

I didn't answer. My chest felt like it was filling with something heavy and light at the same time. She said it so plain, like she was talking about the weather, and it knocked the wind out of me.

We danced until the song ended. Then she kissed my cheek, took a selfie of us making ugly faces, and said, "Wanna ditch early and get slushies?"

I said, "Yes." I would've said "yes" to anything she asked at that moment. If she'd suggested we drive to New York and audition for *America's Got Talent* with a slam poem about sea turtles, I'd have been halfway to the Greyhound station.

We didn't even say goodbye to the others. We just left.

In the gas station parking lot, sipping cherry cola slush through shared silence, I felt weirdly okay. I hadn't died. I hadn't done anything brave, either. But I had moved through something uncomfortable.

Later that night, I lay in bed and wrote a poem that started with, "Your palm was too warm for a lie." Then I crossed it out. Then, I rewrote it as, "I danced like a frog in a tuxedo, and you still looked."

I then watched the sloth poem again.

When it ended, I whispered, "I want to love something with you," into the dark.

And, though I didn't say who "you" was, the creek already knew.

The air felt thinner the next week. Not literally—the barometric pressure was fine—but something had changed in the way people moved. In the hallways, I noticed a recalibration. The girls in art class high-fived me. A boy I didn't know called me "the sleeper cell of dance floors."

Even Cade looked at me differently—less like I was a background character and more like a puzzle with a missing piece he couldn't stop trying to find.

We didn't talk about the dance.

We didn't talk about much at all, actually, until Friday afternoon when I passed him near the gym and he said, "You coming out to the trails later?"

It wasn't a question so much as a tether.

Charlie had a birthday party, so it was just me and Cade. We met by the culvert where the creek elbowed out and looped around the biggest stretch of flat rocks. The thaw had passed, but the water still carried urgency—brown and quick, like it had secrets to move.

Cade had a ziplock of sour candy in one hand and a banged-up Nerf football in the other.

"I brought this," he said, like it explained anything.

We tossed it back and forth for a while, neither of us saying much. The woods were louder than usual—birds reemerging, branches creaking, water dragging itself toward the lake. Cade's throws were lazy but accurate. Mine were too tight, overthought. He didn't seem to mind.

After a while, he sat down on the big rock and pulled at a blade of grass between his fingers.

"I ever tell you my brother broke his collarbone jumping off this?" he asked.

"No," I said, sitting beside him.

"He said it didn't hurt at first. Just felt like someone unplugged his body."

I nodded. "That tracks."

We sat in silence. The creek gurgled beside us like it was rehearsing something.

Cade said, "You ever think about kissing someone?"

My breath snagged.

I didn't move. I didn't look at him.

"Sometimes," I said, as casually as I could.

He nodded. "I think about it too. Like, what it would be like. How you're supposed to know if you're good at it or not."

I glanced at him. He wasn't looking at me—just at the water, eyes narrowed, mouth slack.

He tossed the grass blade into the current. "I kissed a girl in sixth grade. Didn't feel like anything. Just pressure."

I almost asked, "What would you want it to feel like?" But I didn't.

Instead, I said, "I kissed someone at the dance."

He turned to me. "Yeah?"

"Chelsea."

"Oh. Cool."

He said it like it was nothing, but I watched his fingers press into his knee.

"She said I watch you like you're a planet that might hit the Earth," I said before I could stop myself. My heart pounded. She really hadn't said that, but I had thought it, and she might as well have said it. It was true.

His eyes met mine then—really met them.

"I don't know what I'm doing," I added.

"Me either," he said. "I think you're good at keeping secrets."

I laughed, too sharply. "That's a weird compliment."

He shrugged. "You know what I mean."

I did.

The creek surged against the banks. The sky was starting to bruise with evening. We sat so still it felt like we were waiting for instructions.

He reached over slowly and nudged his shoulder against mine.

Not an accident. Not quite on purpose either. Just plausible.

I didn't move away.

Eventually, we walked home in silence. Our feet matched pace without effort.

At the edge of the subdivision, where the trees gave way to the first row of boxy houses, he stopped.

"I won't tell anyone," he said. "About what you said."

I nodded. "I know."

And then he was gone—walking backward at first, then turning, breaking into a jog, hands shoved in his hoodie like he was trying to outrun what we hadn't said.

That night, I didn't write a poem. I just lay on my back and stared at the ceiling, letting it spin. I didn't watch the sloth video. I didn't need to.

The next day, I went back to the creek alone. I stood on the rock and closed my eyes and listened.

The water moved beneath me, sure and unbothered.

It didn't need to speak. It already knew.

East of Venice Street

After Frank O'Hara's "The Day Lady Died"

I push myself out the Venice Street door
blocks away from the hospital where I was born,
        now under its third name,
and lean into my silver Ford.

I whisper down Carlysle, to Outer Drive to
Southfield, and merge on the freeway east.

East is home now. Not Venice Street. Not Michigan
but Pittsburgh and the slanted sidewalks that sometimes
push together so fiercely, they break at the rise.

East of the suburbs that constrict my walk.

East of the family that does not know
what to do with me.

East of lunch and paper plates that hold
two slices of wheat bread,
three pieces of turkey,
and one slab of American cheese

in-between.

Road Trip

Along the eastern thumb
of southern Ohio, the hills
wave an ungloved hand, trees

barely leafed in the late April
dawn. Ahead, an eyebrow cloud
hovers above the brew of storm-

front. Ominous light, puce yellow
and puffed with foreboding, traces
the asphalt lines embroidering

the road to Appalachia. I trace them
with my mind's finger, scribing
out the runic legend: break, broke,

broken. In Charleston, West Virginia,
we cross the Kanawha thrice,
sawing our way into the dark coal

heart of yesterday, lost inside
the exhausted seams of fossilized
hope. Breathing awkward air, we

stutter-chat of useless things, wary
of caving in, of folding dreams into
smaller and smaller horizons.

Deep in the mountains, redbuds blush,
ceding the dirt to rock shelves that gaze,
like me, at your granite indifference,

their disdain thrust in slant-eyed grimace
above the mossy surface. A sweet sob of longing
dangles on the pebbled lip, caressed by water

that trickles down the hillside, cleaving
the adamantine soul of the strongest
stone. Strange, my tears do not.

Breezy Clarity

> *. . . I'd prefer not*
> *to wind up a wind-noise*
> *in an apotropaic graveyard.*
>
> —Jeremy Hoevenaar

Today has gone from breezy clarity peeking between the boughs
    of the lone spruce the old ones who de-rocked the acreage
left in the field that slopes to birch dappling a carpet of sphagnum

    & thumb-high poplars scattered in the lushness my father
would call *peat* to a gray-blue, sopping blanket just now beginning
    to wring itself out. Walt Whitman, you glorious failure,

come on down! The uncut hair of graves does not undulate
    in Murray Hill Cemetery, but damp ferns do bend in the wind
& offer curt nods in the rain. Marie Chandler died at two years,

    ten months & a vanished-into-cracked-slate number of days
in The Year of Our Lord 1812. How to ward off evil? The dust-motes left
    of whomever got laid to rest in a plot where a maple samara

took root in the stony ground & flourished into dense shade
    for a hundred years before someone made it a mossy stump
whose cambium layer stopped pressing in cellular increments

    a lichened, rough-chiseled, blessing-effaced stone nearly prone
can't say. The day, as do many, has cooked me to logic so circular
    the squealing Kingman merry-go-round once more flings me,

Stevie Whositz & Carlo Martelli into a scuffling pile on the gravel.
My Irish great-grandmother taught her surviving children
the virtues of peat moss. Generations later, we learned witch hazel

eases growing pains & oatmeal soaked overnight
in cream & maple syrup sticks to ribs like nothing else.

A Day Long Awaited

1920

Matilde Stoller finished brushing her hair and gathered the long, silver strands in one hand. Deftly braiding the bundle, she twisted the braid in a neat bun and secured it with the hair pins laid out on her dressing table. Her jacket awaited on the back of the chair. Smiling at herself in the mirror, she applied the faintest touch of rouge on her lips and cheeks.

Her husband called out from the downstairs foyer. "Car's ready, Tilde. It's out front warming up."

Their daughter, Liesel, had given Matilde a new cloche hat, burgundy red with a slick, black feather—perfect for her charcoal gray suit. She slipped on the hat and jacket and descended the curving stairs. Her husband kissed her warmly before he settled her fur coat over her suit. "A day long awaited," she murmured. "If only . . ."

"There will be a line, dearest. We need to go."

She took her husband's arm, her mind swirling with memories.

1872

Tilde opened the cedar chest and lifted out Mama's favorite coverlet. Before spreading the lacy, crocheted blanket on her own bed, she buried her face in the folds. Lavender. Her mother, Liesel's, scent. Tilde lightly fingered the sachet packet before placing it back in the chest. Mama had taught her how to sew the little envelopes when she was six. At Mama's side, for the next eight years, Tilde learned how to bake, make soups and stews, stir up dumplings, and a hundred other kitchen and household tasks.

Two years ago, during a warm autumn very like this one, she and Mama picked the fragrant sprigs and made new sachets for all the trunks and closets. Then winter came. The coldest in memory in southwestern New York. Her mother's last winter, before the agonizing birth that would not come, before her mother died.

Papa married Helga the following year. A widow with three small boys, Helga and her children filled the benches of the large trestle table alongside Tilde and her two brothers. Papa sat at the head and blessed their food, which once again boasted thick roasts, stews with dumplings, roasted vegetables, and, after dinner, deep-dish pies or tall, layer cakes. The best part of their now large family dinners was the after-dinner stories and songs.

Papa sings again.

Tilde smoothed the bedding on her dark walnut poster bed, her mother's scent still wafting through the air. Yesterday, as she carried a basket of laundry down the curving stairs, she saw Papa open a small drawer in the hallway desk. He took out one of Mama's handkerchiefs, sniffed it, and slipped it into his pocket. Helga didn't see.

I know he loves her, but he still misses Mama.

Her stepmother was a Godsend. Papa's eyes shined again. He used a soft voice with Tilde's two brothers and Helga's three small boys, and he played games like he used to.

If only he would stop pushing me to marry Herman Stoller.

Tilde's bedroom window looked down on the side yard. Helga was hanging the last of the laundry on the line.

Helga is kind, loving. I'm happy to help.

Tilde thought of all the chores she herself had finished, many before breakfast—stripping all the beds, washing the sheets, feeding the chickens, milking their two cows, and straining the milk into the wide pans in the milk house. And now, with the breakfast dishes washed and put away, she was remaking the beds. For even two women, it was a lot.

When the beds were all finished, Tilde could go outside. She grabbed the picking basket from the screened porch, and caught the door before it slammed behind her. Soon her basket was filled with three cabbages, two large squash, and three bunches of turnips. The vegetables were at their peak and would go well with Helga's roast. The temperatures were falling, and all the family would pick the garden clean before the week was over. The boys had dug and stored ten bushels of potatoes in the root cellar deep into the hillside next to the barn. The rest of the cabbages, squash, carrots, and turnips would join them.

Bang! The screen door slapped back in place as her father stepped off the porch. He crossed the lawn and stopped at the edge of the garden.

"Well, Tilde?" Papa's soft voice caused Tilde to look up.

"Well, what, Papa?"

"I spoke with Herman Stoller this morning. We helped Heinrich fix a broken part on his press." Frederick Hammond paused. "Herman's ready to marry. I told him about that excellent cake you made, all the chores you do."

"Papa, please stop asking me to marry him."

"Matilde," Papa said, his warm tone changing. "Do not continue to disrespect me!"

Tilde took a step back and set down the basket. Keeping her voice low and calm, she said, "But, Papa, how can we marry? I don't even know him, and he doesn't know me either."

She breathed in the garden air, crisp with the dry smells of autumn. Reaching out her hand, she laid it gently on her father's shoulder.

Frederick Hammond shook off Tilde's hand. "You will know him well enough when you're married."

His face stormy, he picked up the basket. "Tilde, listen to me. Herman's a fine, strong lad. Joining our farms will make our future secure. Land will make our family strong. Ours and the Stollers." He turned to go back to the house. Shouting over his shoulder, he said, "Heinrich and I have settled the matter. You will marry Herman Stoller at Yuletide."

Her eyes brimming with tears, Tilde called after him, "Papa, I love you. I mean no disrespect. But I will not be forced to marry. Mama would agree. She would be heartbroken."

He stopped and whirled, his face red with anger. "Your mutter is gone, Tilde. She would expect you to obey as she obeyed her vater to marry me. It is our way."

Tilde didn't wait to hear what else Papa had to say. She ran, lifting her skirts and sprinting up the slope to the apple orchard—her refuge since Mama died.

She pulled herself onto the lower branch of her favorite apple tree. Climbing higher, she nestled close to the trunk, partially hidden from the back garden. Her father's shouts faded in the distance. He wouldn't listen and cared nothing for what she wanted. *Land. It was all Papa thought about, talked about.*

She would not marry Herman Stoller. Not him, not anyone. Papa had talked about marrying her to Herman for months. When she mumbled her excuses that she was not ready, that Helga needed her to help with the household, he usually rushed out to the barn after slamming the door to the back porch. Each time he brought it up, he became more demanding—Tilde must obey, marry, and unite the Stoller and Hammond families, connecting their acres to forge what Papa called a dynasty.

Herman wasn't ugly. He wasn't anything. In all their years growing up on farms that were side by side, Herman had hardly said two words to Tilde. His younger brother Ben was different.

When Mama was alive, Mrs. Stoller had Ben give Mama old issues of the Rochester newspaper and another paper called *The Revolution* established by Susan B. Anthony and Elizabeth Cady Stanton. Tilde read both, cover to cover. Women had the same rights as all citizens. Mama had known this. She shared copies of the women's suffrage paper with Tilde when it was first published in 1868. Tilde had all the copies at the bottom of her trunk. Even after *The Revolution* ceased to print, Tilde and Mama would read over the columns and talk about women having a role in governing. If Papa disagreed, Mama never said.

After Mama died, Tilde had no one to get her the Rochester paper with the news about Miss Anthony and Mrs. Stanton. That is, until one day when Tilde shared with Ben how much she missed reading the news that Mrs. Stoller had passed to Mama. Ben, her one true friend, had slipped Tilde old issues of the *Rochester* weekly paper ever since.

Tilde heard the soft yips of the Stollers' sheep dogs. She scooted around in her tree to better see the Stoller pasture that sloped down next to the Hammond orchard. Ben walked toward the stile, the dogs at his heels.

"I see you, Miss Matilde. Toss me down an apple." Ben jumped down from the stile and fell to his knees. "Please, Miss, I'm plain starving and will never make it back to the fold without one of your sweet, red apples, the Emperor what's-his-name apples."

Tilde laughed. "They're nearly all picked, Ben, but here's one they missed."

She plucked a ripe, ruby-colored apple from the boughs near the branched forks where she sat. "Alexander, Ben. Emperor Alexanders are the eating apples. Most of the others go to the market or are stored for cooking and cider."

Ben took a bite out of the apple she tossed. "Ahh. Just what I needed." He took another bite. "Vater had me clean the press yesterday after they fixed it." He stood and put his foot on the first step of the stile. "He wants to start pressing tomorrow." He chewed another bite. "We had a bit of the old cider left in the spring house. Fizzy."

Tilde laughed again. "You're lucky you didn't get a mouthful of vinegar."

Ben gave her his crooked smile, pushed his sandy curls back under his cap, and bounded up and over the stile. Ben was fourteen, she sixteen. Herman, the eldest, was nearly twenty. Many of the girls in their Lutheran congregation would be happy to marry Herman Stoller and raise a family. But not Tilde.

Tilde waved as Ben signaled the dogs to move the sheep down to the Stollers' barn. She shuddered amid the branches of her hiding place and wiped away her tears. Yuletide! Once her favorite holiday.

Oh, Mama. Christmas isn't the same without you.

Then, another thought intruded.

Could Papa force me to marry Herman on Heilig Abend? Tilde gagged at the thought, slipped down from the tree, and meandered up the fence line to the hickories. The hickories, golden sentinels in the setting sun, rose high on the hill over the farm.

Somehow Tilde had to stop Papa from rushing her into a marriage with Herman. Maybe Papa would soften, let her have more time. If she waited long enough, one of the village girls would catch Herman's eye, and she'd be free of him.

Why does Papa get to decide everything? Even who I marry? What I read? This is America—New York—not Deutschland! And it's 1872!

Sitting on a stump near the hickories, Tilde wondered if Papa would shout at her when she went back to the house.

Helga has a way of calming Papa. Maybe I should wait. Why can't he see times are changing? Women should have lives of their choosing, the right to vote, the right to control their own lives.

* * *

A week before Thanksgiving, despite the snow, worshippers filled the pews at Grace Lutheran Church. The Hammond family's pew was full with Papa, Helga, her sons, and Tilde's two brothers. Tilde slipped in beside Ben in the Stollers' pew. Herman was on his other side next to his small sisters. He glanced her way but said nothing. Ben gave her a grin and slipped a folded newspaper into her hand. As the pastor began the service, Tilde read the headline on the front page of the weekly *Rochester*.

She muffled a gasp. Susan B. Anthony had been arrested! *Why?* She sneaked a look at the text beneath the headline. *For voting? But that had been weeks ago.* Aunt Katharina, her mother's sister, would know more. *Thank goodness she is coming today.* Tilde sighed upon that thought. In her last letter, Aunt Katharina had praised Miss Anthony and the ten other women for voting on November 5. Her aunt would know what else had happened.

* * *

Tilde hurriedly set the table for their midday meal. Her aunt had arrived by train just as their church service had let out.

"Anything else?" Tilde took off her apron when Helga shook her head.

"Go on, your aunt may need help unpacking." She looked at the sink. "Better take up some clean water in case she wants to bathe. Trains are dusty."

Tilde filled one of the large, white pitchers that rested on the sideboard.

Aunt Katharina had stayed in Tilde's room every visit from the time Tilde was little. Long after they blew out the candles, they'd tell each other stories, finally saying goodnight and reciting the prayers Katharina and Liesel had learned as children back in Germany. Tilde had looked forward to the visit by Aunt Katharina for months. She knocked lightly on the door and went in. She set the pitcher on the washstand and, to the surprise of both, burst into tears.

Aunt Katharina held Tilde as she sobbed. "Papa says I must marry."

"I will talk to your Papa, dear heart." Katharina sighed and brushed Tilde's golden curls back from her face.

Katharina poured the fresh water into the basin. Dipping one of the soft cotton cloths into the cool water, she dabbed at Tilde's face until the red splotches softened and disappeared.

"Your skin is just like Liesel's—like Liesel's was—so fair, like peach blossoms." Katharina's own eyes filled. "I miss her beyond words, Liebling. She wished so for you to have a sister. She and I were only two years apart." Katharina sank down on the bed, her face in her hands.

Tilde gently pulled her aunt's hands away. She wet the cloth again and wiped her aunt's face.

"Papa doesn't talk about Mama anymore, but I know he misses her. I saw him tuck one of her handkerchiefs in his pocket. Helga didn't see."

"She is good to you? And the boys?"

"Oh, yes, Auntie. And she loves Papa. I care for her deeply. Papa is happier. It's just his idea about joining our farm with the Stollers." Tilde's voice broke. "Mama wouldn't make me marry someone I hardly know."

"No, she would support you making your own choice." Katharina softened her voice. "It was different when Liesel and I were young. We hadn't been in this country very long. Our parents wanted us settled with good husbands." She took a deep breath. "Your papa is a good man. Liesel loved him. My Johann, too, before he sickened and died, we had grown closer than I ever imagined."

Tilde sat beside Katharina. "Please tell me about Miss Anthony. How could they arrest her weeks later for voting? What is being done?"

"Miss Anthony's supporters say her lawyers will argue that she has the right to vote because she is a citizen, and the Fourteenth Amendment protects a citizen's right to vote. As for the delay, I do not know."

Katharina stood and hung up her traveling clothes. Wiping her face again and then under her arms, she dried with the towel next to the basin. She selected a soft white blouse and gray skirt from her valise. After dressing, she whispered, "A trial may happen, but that is good news. That decision affects us all."

"But Auntie, is Miss Anthony in jail?" The fear in Tilde's voice caused Aunt Katharina to hold her tightly.

After a moment, Tilde stepped back from her aunt's embrace. Clearing her throat, she said, "Please tell me."

Katharina smoothed down Tilde's curls and tucked the wisps back under the braids that circled her loose, flowing tresses. "No, she is free but under constraint by the courts. It is complicated. I suspect a trial will be a first, long step to get women the rights we have under God and the laws of men."

* * *

When Thanksgiving arrived, Katharina spoke during the festive dinner. "Frederick, every young lady wishes for a little adventure before settling into marriage and children. When Liesel brought Tilde to visit with me in Rochester, we went to the orchestra and walked through the beautiful parks. I'm sure she would enjoy another trip before her marriage." She smiled. "Perhaps a new dress might be an early holiday present."

Papa laughed and agreed. The day after the Thanksgiving feast, Tilde and Katharina boarded the train to Buffalo. They would change to another train and be in Rochester by early evening.

The parks, shops, and music might very well happen, but Tilde and Katharina agreed—the most important activity in their minds was to support Miss Anthony by attending her speeches to encourage the right to vote.

And attend they did. All of Rochester was buzzing with revolution-ary energy. Hundreds of women and some men gathered to hear Miss Anthony's fiery speeches. During the end of Tilde's first week at Aunt Katharina's modest house along the Genesee River, the two bundled up in mittens and scarves and walked several blocks to Corinthian Hall. Standing along the right wall in the crowded building, Tilde and her aunt were still close enough to see the smile on Miss Anthony's face as she surveyed the crowd from the podium.

"Friends and fellow citizens," she began in a clear, bell-like voice, "I stand before you tonight, under indictment for the alleged crime of having voted at the last presidential election, without having a lawful right to vote."

She paused and loud murmurs were heard from the crowd. "It shall be my work this evening to prove to you that in thus voting, I not only committed no crime, but instead simply exercised my citizen's right, guar-anteed to me and all United States citizens by the national Constitution, beyond the power of any State to deny."

Loud cheers broke out and several clapped while some waved small flags.

Tilde gripped Aunt Katharina's hand. "She's amazing. I'd love to meet her, to help somehow."

The speech was long, but, except for several moments of clapping and cheers, the audience listened attentively.

On the frosty walk home, Tilde said, "Her last words will stay with me forever, Auntie. 'That we will fight for the ballot peaceably . . . per-sistently to complete triumph, when all United States citizens shall be recognized as equals before the law.'"

* * *

Two weeks passed. Aunt Katharina received a telegram from Tilde's father. It was time to come home.

"Auntie, I can't go back. He'll force me to his will. I want to stay, to help Miss Anthony. Please let me stay." Tilde bit her lip and clung to Katharina's arm.

Katharina took a deep breath. Her brow furrowed. "He'll come here. Take you back."

Tilde sighed and straightened up. "I won't be where Papa can find me. I've looked. Other women will help. There are boarding houses, places to work. What I'd like most is to help with delivering Miss Anthony's tracts. I could deliver to the shops, pass papers out at the rallies. I won't burden you." She burst into tears. "I won't go back."

Katharina sighed and clasped both of Tilde's hands. "All right. I'll write Frederick and tell him you've left my house to work for your own sustenance." She paused, and, once again, held Tilde to her breast. "I'll tell him he should be proud of you, that you are growing into an independent woman who will take care of herself."

* * *

A week before Christmas, Tilde unpacked her valise and put her clothing in the dresser drawer assigned to her. She shared a room with three other chambermaids in the Riggs Hotel. All of the women were older. One, Mary, was even older than Aunt Katharina. Mary gave Tilde a uniform and showed her the linen closet she would access to change the bedding in the rooms. Last on the tour was the tiny room next to the busy kitchen where the staff would eat. Tilde realized she was hungry. The food was plain—beans baked in a molasses sauce, hard bread, and a pitcher of ale. Mary sat beside her and talked about her own life on a farm. When Mary talked about the lambs and baby chicks, Tilde looked away, a tear threatening to spill from her eyes.

"Your family?" Mary asked.

"Two brothers." Tilde cleared her throat. "My father and his wife."

"Ah, I see," Mary said, her voice quiet.

"No, you don't," Tilde said, rising from her seat. "I love them all."

Aunt Katharina had introduced Tilde to the owners of the hotel who were known supporters of Susan B. Anthony. During her free hours late in the afternoon, Tilde took the trolley to Madison Street and Miss Anthony's home. There she and six other young ladies bundled the pamphlets that had been printed for distribution at the evening's rally.

Though she wrote Papa, Helga, and her brothers every week, she received no response.

The morning before Christmas, Aunt Katharina came to the hotel. "I will be in Albany until after the New Year. You remember Johann's brothers and their families are still there. You will be all right?"

"Of course. The hotel will have guests. I'm needed. You should be with your husband's family."

When Katharina returned, Tilde was no longer at the hotel.

"Your young niece was hired away by a friend," Mrs. Riggs explained. "She's sewing for a very exclusive shop, doing alterations as well as creating fancy evening wear. Tilde's attention to detail is exquisite."

"And where is she lodged?" Katharina asked. "I was hoping she'd return with me to my home."

"After you told me her father had come twice to find her, I asked her not to give me the rooming house address. Perhaps, if her father no longer threatens to take her back to the farm, she will stay with you." Mrs. Riggs smiled. "She has choices. For now, I'm sending any mail to Miss Anthony. Your young lady is a regular helper, Miss Anthony says, and is there several times a week."

"Does she get mail from home?" Katharina asked.

Mrs. Riggs paused. "Not from her father, I believe, but sometimes from his wife. Most of her letters seem to be from a young man. Stoller is his last name. When Tilde was here, she wrote to him daily."

1876

Four years later, Tilde received the letter she'd been awaiting. She and Ben had exchanged letters often. But this letter was special. He was coming to Rochester and wanted to see her. She could almost see Ben's smile when he wrote about himself. He was now eighteen and had left the farm to work on the New York Central Railroad. Today, Tilde was to meet him in the coffee shop next to the station on Mill Street.

Ben jumped to his feet when Tilde came through the door.

Tilde laughed and rushed forward. "You're so tall." Ben had shot up to be taller than her father, even Ben's own father, and brother Herman. "Is your father angry?"

He motioned for her to sit. "No, he was at first, but he could see I wasn't really needed. The farm is fine without me. Herman married, you know. He has two sons already."

Tilde reached over the table and laid her hand softly over his. "Katharina told me about Herman. I almost went home for a visit, especially when Helga had her baby." She sighed. "Papa won't speak to me or see me despite Katharina's invitations to come. He blames her even more than he blames me." Clearing her throat, Tilde released Ben's hand. "You chose to live a different life?"

"Yes, I like the railroads, the adventure. Walking behind a mule wasn't the life I wanted. Papa has already forgiven me. He came up and rode on a train to Albany. He was thrilled." Ben leaned forward and wiped a tear from Tilde's cheek. "Your papa will forgive you, too. He just needs more time."

1880

Tilde sat in a rocking chair holding her newborn son. Her young daughter was asleep upstairs when the door chime rang. Her maid answered quickly.

"Is Mrs. Stoller up?" Katharina whispered as she entered.

"Yes, ma'am. Young Liesel is asleep, but the mistress is in the parlor with the baby."

Behind Katharina, Frederick Hammond took off his hat and hung it on the carved oak hall stand. He stood a moment looking into the parlor. "She looks," he paused, his voice choking.

"I know, Frederick. She's the image of our dear Liesel."

"Please come in, Papa, Auntie." Tilde smiled and pulled the blanket slightly back from the baby's face. She spoke to the baby whose eyes were beginning to open, his tiny fist searching for his mouth. "Little Heinrich, wake up to meet your grandfather."

Frederick stepped forward and kissed Tilde on her forehead. He touched the baby's head, a solitary tear leaking down his cheek.

"Papa, I'm so glad you've come. Please sit so I can slide him into your arms. Ben and I named him Heinrich Frederick Stoller for both of his grandfathers." She stood and, after her father sat on the settee, placed the baby in his arms.

"Tilde," Frederick began. He stroked the baby's cheek with his finger. "I am sorry. I should have come before—when the little girl was born, when you and Ben were married. Heinrich and Hannah have scolded me repeatedly." He hung his head, the baby staring up at him.

"He is very handsome," Papa said, his voice quiet. He looked up at Tilde and said tenderly, "And you—you are very beautiful, my daughter."

"Papa," Tilde's voice broke. "I am filled with happiness."

She sat beside her papa and newborn son. She put her arms around them and kissed Papa on his cheek. "Ben's train will be in at half past four. We'll have supper at six."

Looking at Katharina, she said, "You'll stay, of course."

"Certainly, and tomorrow for tea Miss Anthony and Mrs. Stanton will join us."

Frederick looked startled for a moment. "Tilde, are you sure my visit is not an imposition? You have the room?"

"Yes, Papa. You will sleep in the room over the library. Ben's father and mother stay there quite comfortably. We have a cook now, and dinner will be a real celebration. Papa," Tilde couldn't speak.

Papa took her hand. "I never stopped loving you."

1920

"Take my hand, Ben. I feel shaky today."

"You've waited almost fifty years for this day. I would be surprised if you weren't shaky." Ben put his arm around Tilde's shoulder. "I'm excited, too, dearest one."

Tilde laughed and pointed. "Look, Liesel is here ahead of us." She waved her handkerchief at their daughter.

The line wound from the courthouse nearly to the park. Women of all ages, shapes, and sizes chatted and smiled. Some were accompanied by their menfolk, but many were alone, standing tall and proud. Most of the younger women like Liesel wore the newest frocks with a dropped waist and a cloche hat over their bobbed hair.

Holding Ben's hand tightly, Tilde said, "I wish Katharina had lived to see this day. She and Miss Anthony traveled clear across the country."

"I know, darling. I remember her well. A strong woman, your aunt."

Ben guided Tilde up the courthouse steps. Liesel had disappeared inside. Just as Ben and Tilde reached the doors, Liesel came out waving a small flag.

"America is truly my country now," Liesel shouted, her words not only for her parents but for the gathered crowd. A cheer went up, both men and women celebrating this longed-for day.

Tilde hugged her daughter tightly. "Our country. Our freedoms—finally. One Nation under God, with liberty and justice for all."

"Come to dinner, Mama, Papa. Charles's train arrives at three. He'll vote before he drives home."

Tilde kissed Liesel on her cheek. "We would love to. We'll come early to see the children before they go to bed. They're too young to know how special this day is, but they will. One day, you'll tell them."

"Of course, Mama. I'll tell them about Miss Anthony, Mrs. Stanton, you and Great Aunt Kat. They need to know their freedoms did not just happen."

Ben opened the door to the courthouse. "It's time, Tilde. Let's go vote."

Tilde took his arm and reached to caress his hand. "For Mama and Auntie," she breathed and wiped a tear away. "And for Liesel's little girls. For all women. For America."

Flew

O coveted parakeet,
college consigned you to a bathroom
which might still smell like her
if it didn't smell so much like you.

At least you lived your last overlooking
the road where she left. There, we
shared the vacant ache of time behind us
holding those ambrosial moments*

*that day of the open window
when she was still naive enough to sit
so long beneath the trees with hope
and a pillowcase

You flew then too,
didn't you.

Giving Directions

A visitor asks for directions to Murdoch Farms,
she wants to see the "fancy homes,"
I can't remember the exact street, so I say:
    go straight, make a right at CVS,
    all the way up Wightman towards Forbes,

past the large white house where 30 years ago,
    a teenage girl was pierced to death
    by a katana at 3 a.m.,
    having let in her drug-addled friend
    by disabling the security system.

The neighbors heard her cries, but no one came to help.

I was at a party when I heard the news,
    tremors,
I couldn't sleep all night that night—
    imagine the surgeon father trying to resuscitate his broken child,
    the wild-haired mother who couldn't scream . . .

be sure to make that right before you reach Forbes—
    that's the place you want—
    the fanciest homes you ever saw.

Reasons with Examples

I.
A girl lay unconscious outside of a bar at night.
Her golden hair knotted in broken
glass and cigarette butts.
I thought she was dead,
and all I did was stare.
When she groaned, I took her phone number—
but not until she groaned.

II.
I am a ghost haunted by a house.
I call my father to give him something
to pick up.

III.
I scraped the live skin cells off of my hand.
When my body had repaired itself,
I did it again,
just out of spite.

IV.
My sister told me that if I put the gum in my mouth,
I would walk to school—
When I finally arrived, I stuck the gum
to the pages of books,
wet from the pouring rain.

V.
I didn't tell anyone about it,
and now I cannot uncurl my fingers.
I didn't tell anyone about it,
and now I cannot unclench my teeth.
Blood drips from my nose and I cannot wipe it.

VI.
I tell her that I'll go with her to get help,
but I sit in the bathroom instead.

VII.
I like the way the tape
peels the paint off the wall.

VIII.
I like the way the gulls run when I chase them.

IX.
My sister forgives me for the gum.
I do not forgive her for the books.

X.
The girl made it home safe, but I did not
walk her there.

Third Weekend in March

Still time for the fireplace before sunrise.
Then coffee on the deck. You notice winter,
pry barred some pickets from the fence, exposed
dog-tooth nails. You think another cup,
then ceramic screws at the hardware store—
and Ohio Blue Tip Matches.
                                        The book says
now is when to lop the Rose of Sharon.
In this climate, we cut them to our knees
as if every measure were always about us—
a pretty thing to think, until you think
of someone else.
                              How your oldest brother
on the last night whispered in your mother's ear:
Tomorrow it turns spring. A good day to die.
Now, he is gone too. You won't be old men,
dirty-legged in the wrong-length shorts,
arguing bloodroot and violets.
                                            You'll take the pup
who is welcome there to wander the aisles.
The clerk will pet him and opine upon the screws.

Lookout Farm

Past rustled rows that stalk a moonless night
the tractor ruts return to the old barn
where Cervelli's talking to himself.

Chore lights make his shadow dance
on the walls, where whinnying gusts
stir ragweed, pine pollen dust.

The massive sliding door is rolled ajar.
Inside the yolk-and-scythe museum's
centerpiece is a gigantic rope swing—

Clasping the rope, he leans into the dark,
recalling in his youth he swung aloft,
before planting both feet firmly on the earth.

The barn is more than a discarded husk,
it is an ark survived another flood
upon a hill where kernels of hope keep

Cervelli from cementing his farm's well.

The Actor

Will Travers threw two heavy trash bags over his shoulder and started walking down the main pathway through the quad toward the maintenance truck. He thought of the conversation he'd had with his buddies a day or two before he'd started this job. They teased him about working at the college, called him "professor," and suggested he try to sleep with one or two students. "It's a target-rich environment," one of them had said. "You shouldn't have any trouble hooking up." He had laughed, but very quickly found that no such fate awaited him. The girls didn't notice him; neither did the boys for that matter. He passed through their ranks like a ghost, an invisible man. One afternoon, as if to underscore the point, a lime green frisbee whizzed past his head. He saw it out of the corner of his eye and felt the breeze as it passed. He heard laughter, and he knew the young men and women were laughing at him; he sensed they didn't see a person there, only a symbol of the college's hidden functions—the things that kept life there humming along with comforting regularity. He put his head down and quickened his pace, and within a few seconds, he was at the truck. He tossed the bags in the back, climbed into the driver's seat, fired up the engine, and headed toward the buildings and grounds department.

He threw the bags in the dirty green dumpster behind the low slung building, turned in the keys, stripped off his work clothes, showered, dressed, and clocked out. At a little past 5 o'clock, he was on his way to the Buffalo Inn, a ramshackle bar on the edge of town that served both locals and students alike.

On this particular evening, the bar was nearly deserted. Will ordered a beer and lit a cigarette. Rules against smoking indoors were loosely enforced—as loosely as were those against underage drinking. Will took a drag and a sip of his beer and watched ESPN out of the corner of his eye. A couple of talking heads were debating the relative strengths and weaknesses of that weekend's lineup of college teams, and a scrolling chyron beneath their torsos showed the latest sports news. Neil Diamond was on the jukebox singing "Sweet Caroline," and the metal beer signs and dusty pennants on the wooden walls gave off a comforting feeling. Will finished his first beer and ordered another, settling into a pleasant buzz.

After a few minutes, Will noticed another man sitting at the bar, almost directly across from him. This man did not look like a student or a townie. For one thing, he was much older, around forty-five or fifty years old, and he was clean shaven with a thick head of heavily-gelled black hair. He had a deep dimple in his chin and a tanned complexion, as though he had recently returned from an extended vacation somewhere expensive. He wore a pink sports jacket over a black silk polo shirt and a pair of bright blue chinos. He looked like one of the talking heads on ESPN, but with a hint of menace, as though he had done bad things in his past and could do them again. When he signaled for another drink, Will caught a glimpse of a titanium Rolex Yacht-Master on his thick wrist.

The man, seeing that Will had noticed him, gave him a wink and a nod. When his drink came—a Manhattan—he stood up from his stool and walked over to Will.

"Paul Trevino," he said, extending a meaty hand toward Will.

"Will Travers," Will said.

"May I sit?" Trevino said, gesturing toward the neighboring bar stool.

"Be my guest."

"Mountaineers are looking good this season," Trevino said, nodding toward the TV where the talking heads were discussing WVU.

Will just shrugged.

The two men sat in silence for a while as they watched the sports newscast. The bar began to fill up. Someone put Led Zeppelin on the jukebox. "Ramble On" came through the speakers. The kitchen began to crank out orders of french fries and chicken wings. Trevino took out a newspaper clipping and showed it to Will.

"You the Will Travers mentioned in this article?" he asked, placing the clipping in front of Will and taking a sip of his drink.

Will took a look at the story. It was from that spring.

The headline said, "Handyman Saves Horses After Barn Fire."

"Yeah, that's me," he said, taking another sip of his beer and pushing the clipping back toward Trevino.

"Quite a thing you did," Trevino said.

"Guess so," Will said.

"Saving all those horses."

"Wasn't nothing, really."

"Tell me what happened," Trevino said.

"Look, mister," Will said, turning to Trevino. "I don't mean to be rude, but you can read the story for yourself in the paper. I guess you have already. I don't see the point of me repeating it for you."

"I guess I should introduce myself," Trevino said.

"I thought you just did," Will replied.

"I mean properly," Trevino said. "I represent Connor McLennon. You know him?"

"The actor?"

"That's right."

"Shit, I guess I do," Will said. "He's only the most famous person to come out of this valley in the last twenty years—him and Brad Paisley. Sure, I know about him."

"Did you know he owns some land around here?"

"I heard something about that," Will said. "He bought the old Wilson farm, right?"

"About ten years ago," Trevino said. "Fixed it up real nice. Big main house with a pool, a guest house, tennis courts, a dirt racing track, and stables——a dozen horses in all, a couple of them thoroughbreds."

"That's great," Will said. "Good for him. He's done good, I guess."

"Yes," Trevino said. "He's been very successful. Single-handedly brought westerns back, you might say. And he just signed on to do a string of action movies. Old school stuff. Not that superhero crap."

"That's great," Will said, a little less enthusiastically. "God bless."

The two men fell silent again. Will could tell there was something Trevino wanted to ask him though he seemed to be unable to find the right words.

"Listen," Trevino finally said. "I was wondering if you could do us a favor?"

"Us?" Will said.

"Well, yes," Trevino said. "Me and Mr. McLennon."

"Connor?"

"Yes, Connor," Trevino said.

"What's the favor?" Will asked, concentrating on his beer.

"Well, you see, our caretaker recently left abruptly, and we're in a bit of an awkward position, I'm afraid. He took care of the grounds and the horses, and without him, we're in a real jam. I've been taking care of the horses for the last week, and, believe me, I'm no cowboy."

"You don't say."

"It's been a little rough."

"Why'd he leave?"

"Got a job with an oil and gas outfit if you can believe that."

"Sure," Will said. "Good money."

"Of course," Trevino said. "I can't blame him for that. He's got a family and everything. Still, the simple fact of the matter is that he's left us in a really difficult position. We need to find someone fast. We were hoping you might be interested in the job."

"Why me?"

"It says here that you saved three horses from a fire after the stables were hit by lightning in April. And that you rounded up the others before the people who ran the place could even get on site, including the full-time trainer."

"No big deal," Will said, shrugging. "My apartment's right next to the place. I know a few of the basics, so what? I don't know nothin' about thoroughbreds."

"There's not much to know, as I understand it," Trevino said. "Anyway, I'm sure you're a quick study."

"Maybe," Will said. "But how do I know you're not gonna can my ass as soon as someone with more experience comes along? I got a good job here, you know."

"I understand," Trevino said. "But I wouldn't worry about that. McLennon says he wants you. Knew it the minute he read this item in the paper. Don't ask me why."

"Guess I'm pretty lucky then," Will said.

"Look," Trevino said. "Why don't you come up tomorrow and have a look around and decide for yourself. The job pays sixty grand a year plus room and board. That's gotta be better than you're doing here."

"I do alright."

"I'm sure you do," Trevino said. "No question. But just think about it, okay? Here's my card. Call me when you decide."

Trevino handed Will a thick business card with his name printed on the front and his cell phone number written on the back. He finished his drink, wiped his mouth with a cocktail napkin, and put a fifty dollar bill on the bar. Then he stood up, straightened his pink jacket, and said, "Nice talking with you," before walking out of the Buffalo Inn.

"Nice talking to you too," Will said to no one in particular.

That night, Will dreamt there was a big party in his apartment. The place was packed with people, and the crowd spilled out into the hall. The bass line to a rap song was thumping against the walls and shaking the whole building. There were cans of beer and red plastic cups strewn across the floor. Someone was puking in the bathroom. In the corner, a huge machine, part metal and part biologic, bucked and hissed, throwing off noxious fumes. It seemed on the verge of breaking down. Slowly, almost imperceptibly at first, the walls of the apartment started closing in and elongating, forming a kind of tunnel. The whole room tilted on its axis and angled sharply up. The floor and walls turned to hard-packed mud covered by loose dirt and rubble; the light at the end of the tunnel became harder to see. People began stampeding over one another to get out.

Will began crawling up toward the light, but he was pulled back. People were climbing over him, stepping on his face to get a purchase on the loose soil ahead, and he was stepping on people too, pushing them farther down into the tunnel as he tried to get out. The small circle of light at the end of the tunnel began to close, and he found it harder and harder to breathe. He could taste the rubber of someone's dirty shoe, then felt the soil of the tunnel fill his mouth. It felt rich and black, like chocolate cake, but there was too much of it, and he began to choke. He tried to cough, but no sound or air came out. He tried to swallow, but his mouth filled up again. The cake tasted like dirt and grass, and there were tiny stones in it that chipped his teeth. And just as he was about to surrender—to let the earth overtake him, to let it bury him alive—he woke up in a cold sweat in his tiny, empty apartment and gasped for air.

It was a Saturday morning, almost half past eleven. He got out of bed, filled a glass of water at the sink, and drank it greedily. Then he picked up Trevino's card, called him, and said he would take the job.

* * *

The actor's farm was located on a low ridge between two opposing hills. Beyond it, the Appalachian mountains rose and rolled into the distance. The entrance to the farm, which comprised about 300 acres, was hidden by a thickly wooded knoll off the main road. Will had nearly missed it the first time he showed up for work. The main house was a large, low-slung building built to resemble a western lodge with a lot of glass and raw timber beams. Behind it stood a guest house that looked like an Alpine ski chalet. The incongruous design was meant to reflect the actor's two main interests: horses and skiing. There was a pool and a hot tub, a roundabout driveway paved with granite setts, and a fishing pond. The stables were located down a sloping path that led away from the house. Twenty stalls, ten on each side, held only twelve horses. Each occupied stall was emblazoned with the name of the horse that resided within.

True to what Trevino had told him, there were two thoroughbreds which the actor had purchased after they'd had some success on the racing circuit—big beautiful animals with chestnut hair and regal bearing, delicate in their need for a certain type of feeding and care, and temperamental when they didn't get it. The rest of the horses were typical of what you might find on a hobby farm: three quarter horses, a roan, a dappled gray, an Appaloosa that was said to be the actor's favorite, two ponies, and two grade horses named Sylvia and Charlie who had no particular pedigree. Of all the horses in the stable, Will got along best with Charlie. There was a certain melancholic cast to his big dark eyes, and he greeted Will every morning with an appreciative grunt and a nuzzle so that Will began to perceive a certain wisdom in his bearing.

Will's routine at the farm was fairly straightforward. Each morning he rose before dawn, prepared his breakfast, ate, and headed down to the stables. He fed and watered the horses, brushed out their coats, and checked for signs of disease or illness. A veterinarian came around once a week to assist in their care, but they were healthy animals and usually had no issues. After that was taken care of, Will would turn his attention to various other projects on the farm. He would work inside the house if there was something that needed to be addressed, or outside, cleaning the pool, testing the doors, cleaning the gutters, or painting and making small repairs. Occasionally, a handyman or a delivery truck driver would arrive, and Will would let them in or sign for a package. Once, he had to install a brand new espresso machine that arrived unannounced. The task took him half the morning and the better part of the afternoon.

At least once or twice a week, he would saddle Charlie and ride along the miles of fence that lined the property, looking for weak spots and places that needed to be fixed. His work kept him busy during the day, but his evenings were largely free. After about four or five o'clock in the afternoon, there was nothing much left to do. Will would make his dinner in the main house sometimes just for a change of scenery, and then he would watch the sun set over the hill behind the pool. The nights were peaceful—if a bit lonely. Sometimes, Will would head down to the Buffalo Inn for a beer or two, but mostly he occupied his time with reading. The main house and guest house were both well stocked with books and old magazines, and Will worked his way through them one volume at a time. There were westerns and detective stories and horse magazines and copies of the classics of literature. Will had no idea whether the actor had amassed this collection himself or simply hired someone to do it for him. Its contents seemed to align with whatever his interests might be, but Will could still get no sense of the man.

One morning in late February, Will saddled Charlie and went for a ride over the hills directly behind the house. He had no particular agenda in mind. The fences had been mended, and there were no other issues to address. You could say he wanted to get a better sense of the land, but what he really wanted to do was to get outside himself—get away from himself—to leave his routine behind, to escape into nature, and to feel that momentary release when the body and the mind merge with the wider world as the usual barriers break down. He'd had another disturbing dream the night before and slept fitfully afterward. He hoped to tire himself out enough to sleep well, without dreams, just a black abyss surrounding him. He guided Charlie up a path that led through an old graveyard, a family plot, and then down through a small hollow. Snow still hung around in portions of the field, and the grass was matted and straw-colored. A stream flowed swiftly in the background, and the air was cold and damp. Will and Charlie rode on and eventually came to a ridge overlooking the entire valley. Will could see for miles. The sun broke through the clouds and shone down on farms and school houses and churches, and in the distance old factories and abandoned row houses. Will surveyed the scene and thought about what had happened to him. Two years ago, he'd been in a bad coal mining accident. He'd been assigned to move a waterline and power pack inside one of the shafts when the roof caved in, trapping him and three other miners. Just before it fell, Will had gotten spooked and jumped under a mechanized scoop. When the roof fell, he'd been spared, but the other three miners were killed. They were close to him. He knew them well, and he couldn't forgive himself for surviving when they did not.

That evening he received a call from his estranged wife, Mary Beth. She asked him how he was doing. She told him she'd called the college and had been told he no longer worked there. She chastised him for not telling her about the move himself. They talked for a few more minutes, and she asked him if she could come visit him. Will said he wasn't ready yet. In his mind, he saw the night of their wedding, how they'd danced to "I Swear" by John Michael Montgomery, how they'd smashed cake into each other's faces, and how they'd been surrounded by family. As he was thinking of all this, he began to get dizzy. He squeezed his eyes shut and held his breath. He saw the roof of the mine coming down again and told Mary Beth he had to go.

"Okay," she said. "Have a good night, I guess."

"Thank you," he said.

"Everyone here misses you."

Will said nothing in reply.

"Don't you want to see your son?" she said.

"I do," Will said. "Of course I do. I'm just not ready yet."

"Okay, Will," Mary Beth said. "You be sure to let me know when you are ready, okay?"

"Okay."

"Good night, then."

"Good night."

* * *

One night a few weeks later, Will was having a beer down at the Buffalo Inn when he happened to catch an item on TMZ about the actor. The news had apparently been in all the papers and all over social media, but Will hadn't heard anything about it. The reporter on the TV said that Connor McLennon and his equally famous wife, Camilla Parker, were going through a trial separation. The circumstances surrounding the separation were salacious and included allegations of cheating and drug abuse on the part of McLennon. There was even a suggestion that he had been verbally and physically abusive toward his wife and their three children. The reporter said that Parker was taking the children with her while McLennon's whereabouts were unknown. The images on screen showed a pretty young woman with dark hair wearing large sunglasses and shepherding her children into an oversized black SUV. Then the screen switched to a group of paparazzi questioning McLennon outside an LA restaurant a few days prior to the news. McLennon was wearing a leather jacket over a white western-cut, button-down shirt and a pair of faded Wranglers with cowboy boots. He wore sunglasses, and his sandy blond hair looked matted and dirty. He seemed unsteady on his feet. He was fumbling with his car keys, and when a photographer approached him to ask a question about his wife, McLennon grabbed the man's camera and threw it to the ground. He got into his pickup truck and pulled away from the curb, smashing the back end of a Mercedes sedan and stopping traffic as he pulled a U-turn on Sunset. The segment closed with a shot of the host taking a sip of his coffee, shaking his head, and saying, "You hate to see it."

Will finished his beer, paid his tab, and went back to the guest house. He slept fitfully that night, wondering whether the actor's recent travails would affect his employment, but he heard nothing in the immediate aftermath of the report and continued about his business as usual.

One morning about three days later, three black SUVs arrived at the property. Will watched as McLennon got out of the middle SUV and went into the main house, followed closely by two security guards and Trevino the manager—the man he had met at the Buffalo Inn a few months before, the man who had first offered him his job.

Will continued about his chores, glancing up every so often at the house to see what was happening. After about 20 minutes, Trevino came out of the house and walked down the sloping path toward the stable. Will stopped what he was doing and stood with his flat-head shovel in his hands, watching Trevino come toward him. He was wearing a pastel blue sports coat this time instead of a pink one, but he had the same black polo underneath.

"Howdy," he said as he approached.

"Hello," Will said.

"The place looks great," Trevino said. "You really worked wonders."

"No problem," Will said.

"Listen," Trevino said, scratching the back of his head. "As I'm sure you can appreciate, we've got a bit of a situation here. You don't mind staying on, do you?"

"No, not at all."

"Good," Trevino said. "That's good. I'm glad to hear it. Just keep doing what you've been doing. We'll take care of the rest."

"Okay."

"There's one other thing," Trevino said, kicking at the ground with his nine hundred dollar Salvatore Ferragamo loafers. "It's a bit awkward. I hope you won't mind my bringing it up."

"What is it?" Will said.

"Well, I'm sure I don't need to remind you to be discreet about your work here."

"No," Will said.

"Right," Trevino continued. "And I know you have been—and we appreciate that—but with this thing here now . . . look, I'd just like to remind you, okay? I hope you won't be offended."

"No, it's okay."

"Great," Trevino said, patting Will on the shoulder. "I knew I could count on you. Here's a little something to show our appreciation."

Trevino handed Will a check for five grand. Will folded it and put it in his shirt pocket.

"Thanks," he said.

"You're welcome," Trevino said, unsure of what to do next. "Well, I guess I'll be going. See you around, kid. And thanks again."

"You're welcome," Will said, watching Trevino walk back up the path toward the house.

Several days went by. Will saw very little of McLennon himself, though the place was abuzz with talk of the actor's presence. The quiet rhythm of Will's life on the farm had been interrupted. In the morning, he was awoken by the crackle and static of the security guards' radios, and he could smell their cigarettes and aftershave from his bedroom window as they stood around waiting for their assignments. A whole new crew of workmen, designers, and consultants paraded into and out of the house—all overseen by Trevino's watchful eye. The pool area was given a careful cleaning, and truckloads of food and beverages were brought in to feed the actor and his entourage. A new flatscreen TV was installed, and the home's data and communication systems were upgraded. All the windows were cleaned, and the roof was re-inspected. During this time, Will was largely ignored, but he found it difficult to go about his chores. The horses were disturbed by the new activity, and the security guards eyed him suspiciously.

After a few weeks, things began to quiet down. The deliveries and improvements to the house stopped, and the consultants and security detail went away. The last to leave was Trevino; he merely waved to Will from his rented SUV as he drove off the property. Finally, it was just Will and McLennon. Will saw very little of the actor in the days following the departure of his entourage. He would occasionally catch glimpses of him walking around the house or smoking shirtless on his balcony, his naked torso covered with tattoos. But, other than that, it was like he was not there at all.

* * *

One morning, as Will was working in the stables, he became aware of a presence behind him. He turned around to discover McLennon standing there. The actor walked over and started petting one of the horses.

"Beautiful animals, aren't they?" he said.

"Yes," Will said. "You have some nice ones here. It's been a real pleasure taking care of them."

"You've done an excellent job," McLennon said. "I've never seen them so happy."

"Thank you," Will said. "It's nice to finally meet you."

"It's good to meet you too. Listen, I'm sorry I've been such a recluse. I'm just going through a lot at the moment, as I'm sure you've probably heard."

"No worries."

"Why don't you come up to the house tonight and have a drink or something?"

"Sure," Will said, not knowing what else to say. "I'd like that."

When Will showed up at the main house that evening, it was clear McLennon had made a hasty effort to clean things up. There was still a sticky residue on the coffee table where something had spilled. A large bong sat on the floor beside one of the couches, and on the TV stand, a stray bottle of beer sat empty. On the sideboard was a beautifully crafted jewel box with an ornate lid. Will opened it while McLennon was in the kitchen fixing their drinks. Inside, he discovered half a gram of heroin along with two syringes still sealed in their plastic wrapping. A third was behind the sideboard, unwrapped and used.

McLennon reappeared after a few minutes with two margaritas which he said he made with his own brand of mezcal. He handed one to Will and told him to head out onto the patio while he grabbed a couple of steaks for the grill. The weather was cool but pleasant. It was late spring, and the dogwood trees around the pool were beginning to blossom. The sun was setting, and the sky was a million shades of red and yellow and purple and blue. A northern cardinal flew down from one of the pine trees lining the ridge and landed on the table near the pool. It moved its nervous head around in the twilight, looked at Will for a split second, and flew back into the forest. The fountain near the pool burbled, and a breeze swept down the hill and loosened a few flowers from their branches. They floated across the pool on the breeze and landed in the deep end next to the diving board. Will wondered who would clean them up.

McLennon emerged from the house with two thick-cut T-bone steaks which he had seasoned with salt and pepper. McLennon placed the steaks upright on the wood-fired grill and walked over to where Will was sitting with his drink.

"Cheers," McLennon said, and they touched glasses. The heavy crystal sparkled in the setting sun. The salt on the rims looked whiter than white against the dark flecks here and there.

"Cheers," Will said, taking a sip of his drink. It was strong, mostly alcohol. He sat on an Adirondack chair and watched McLennon cook the steaks. As the sun disappeared over the ridge, a series of automatic lights around the patio and in the pool came on. McLennon burned himself a couple of times on the grill; he finished cooking the steaks after about 10 minutes and then let them rest a few minutes longer. It got colder on the patio, and Will shivered as he finished his margarita.

"Let's eat inside," McLennon said, gesturing with the plate of steaks toward the sliding glass door. Will opened it, and they went inside.

They ate mostly in silence, but began to talk once they were finished with the meal. McLennon told Will what it was like growing up in the valley in the seventies and eighties—how he went to Hollywood on a dare, intending to be a musician; how he was discovered in a dive bar one night by a talent agent who thought he should be a male model; how he started writing scripts and acting on the side; and of his first commercial, his first TV gig, and his first movie. His first million. Then he got into screenwriting, producing—being involved even more with the creative process. He got married and had kids, but the pressure was intense.

"Everybody always wanted something from you," McLennon confessed. "The studios, the agents, the fans, the press. By the time you got home, you had nothing left to give. You know, all the old cliches," he continued. "So you start drinking to numb the pain. You start taking drugs to stay awake. And once you get on that cycle, brother, there ain't no getting off."

Will listened with interest but didn't say much. Every once in a while, as he was telling his tale of woe, McLennon would excuse himself to go to the bathroom. Will could tell he was snorting cocaine in there. After every trip, he returned with a fresh burst of energy, touching his nose and running his tongue over his gums. Will began to get tired. He thought of his chores in the morning and asked McLennon if it would be alright if he excused himself for the evening. McLennon offered him another drink, but when he mentioned the horses, the actor said he understood. He asked Will if he could come down and help in the morning. Will told him it wasn't necessary, but it was his property; he could do what he liked. McLennon said he would be there in the morning, and he was.

The pattern continued for several weeks. Will and McLennon would work with the horses during the day and have dinner together at night. They became friendly and exchanged stories about growing up in the valley, crazy stunts they and their friends had tried, girls they'd bedded, and the ones who'd broken their hearts. They talked about cars and music and movies and discovered they had a lot in common. They became friends.

One evening in June, Will walked up to the main house and knocked on the door. No one answered. As he waited, he heard a great commotion inside. It sounded as though someone was throwing furniture around. Metallica was blaring from the expensive speakers inside, and Will could hear glass breaking. He knocked again but got no answer. He walked around to the patio but didn't see anyone. Eventually, he gave up and went back to the guest house. The music continued thumping through the night, and Will worried that McLennon may have overdosed or committed suicide or met some other ignoble end. He stayed up late and stared at the ceiling. Eventually, around three or four o'clock in the morning, the music stopped, and he passed out. When his alarm went off at six, he felt as though he hadn't slept at all.

A couple of days later, McLennon showed up at the guest house. His eyes were red around the rims, and his hair was wet from the shower. He looked like he hadn't slept or eaten in days. He wore a tank top and a pair of faded jeans and rested his arm against the door jamb as he spoke to Will. He apologized for being incommunicado and invited Will back down to the main house for dinner. He said he was going to make a couple of pizzas in the new pizza oven. Will agreed to come, and they made plans to see each other later that day.

When Will arrived at the house, he saw that McLennon was already drunk and high. The actor kept burning himself on the pizza oven and muttering curses. Will managed to pry him away from the oven and get him to sit down on one of the chaise lounges on the patio near the pool. He went inside, found a blanket, and covered McLennon with it. He finished cooking the pizzas, and when he looked up from his work, he discovered that McLennon had fallen asleep. He was cleaning up from dinner when the actor woke up and came into the kitchen.

"Thanks," McLennon said.

"No problem," Will replied.

"I'm sorry I've been such a mess lately. It's just that, well, you know, Camilla wants a divorce."

"I didn't know that."

"Yeah, sole custody, too. She'll likely get it."

"Will you contest?" Will asked.

"Yeah, but there won't be any point," McLennon said. "You might as well know it. I've been a real bastard. Abusive. All that shit. Everything you read in the press. It's all true."

"I haven't read anything," Will said.

"Ha!" McLennon said. "I guess that's why I like you. You don't pay attention to any of that shit, do you?"

"Not really."

"That's good."

The two men fell silent for a while. Will continued washing the dishes and cleaning up from supper. McLennon picked at a pizza that was on the table.

"My dad was a real bastard too," he finally said.

"Really?" Will said.

"Shit, yeah. He used to beat the shit out of all us kids back in the day. He was a real mean drunk. Finally sobered up, 'bout the time I turned eighteen. Found Jesus. But the damage was already done. Why do you think I took off for Hollywood?"

"I'm not sure," Will said, turning off the faucet and wiping down the counter. "I thought it was a dare."

"Shit man, the dare was just an excuse. I was dying to get away from all that."

"I can understand," Will said.

"Yeah?" McLennon replied. "You have a mean daddy too?"

"Not really," Will said. "Actually, I never knew my father. He took off before I was born. But my momma was a mess. I haven't seen her since I was about seven or eight. No, I was raised by my aunt and uncle. That's actually how I came to know so much about horses. They had a farm like this. Well, not exactly like this, but same idea."

"Really?" McLennon said, genuinely interested.

"Yeah," Will said. "Travers Farm and Faith Ranch. My aunt and uncle both ran it. My uncle was a good man, a strong man, a gentle man, you know? He was an electrician in the mines. Bought the farm back in the seventies. On weekends, and when he was laid off, he would do horse rides for kids and wagon rides—picnics, lessons, stuff like that. He never made much money from it, but he kept it going. He died, though."

"Shit, I know a few people out west who make a pretty penny working with horses, training 'em, teaching kids how to ride in equestrian shows, whatnot. I could probably hook you up."

"That's okay," Will said.

"Just let me know," McLennon said.

"Will do," Will said.

The men were silent again. Outside on the lawn above the pool, fireflies danced in the darkness. The water sparkled, and a whippoorwill called out. McLennon pushed the pizza around on the table, and Will leaned against the sink with his arms folded and looked out at the backyard. After a while, McLennon spoke again.

"You said your uncle died?"

"Yeah," Will said.

"How did he die?"

"He was killed in the mines," Will said.

"Oh," McLennon said.

"My best friend, too."

"I'm sorry," McLennon said.

"It's okay," Will said.

And then, without really meaning to, Will told him the whole story—how his uncle and his best friend and brother-in-law, Jordan, had been assigned to move some stuff around the mine; how he had been out late the night before with Jordan; how they'd had a bump or two in the morning to stay awake; how he'd nodded off on the man trip and been foggy-headed and less than totally diligent while checking the roof supports; how he'd gotten a strange kind of sixth sense before anything happened and moved closer to the mechanized scoop they were using to move some equipment around; how his uncle had shoved him under the metal canopy when he heard the roof start to give way and then called for Jordan to come running; and how a huge section of the roof (thirty feet wide by fifty feet long) finally gave way, crashing down on the miners.

He'd been saved by the scoop, saved by his uncle, and in the silence of the aftermath, all he'd heard was a fervent prayer that went nowhere, trapped in the deep earth and choked by stale earth and rock dust. It took him a minute or two to realize it was coming from his lips. Then he stopped. There was nothing left to say. The mine had said it all.

Will told McLennon that he was cleared of any wrongdoing by the ensuing investigation, but he just couldn't forgive himself for surviving when the others had not. Each night, before he fell asleep, the whole scenario played out in his head again, and he questioned everything. Sometimes he blamed his uncle. He was the far more experienced miner. Why hadn't he picked up on anything? Sometimes he blamed his brother-in-law. Why had Jordan dragged him out the night before to complain about his latest girlfriend? But, mostly, he blamed himself. Why hadn't he said something? Why hadn't he done a better job checking the roof supports? Why hadn't he asked his uncle for his opinion on the condition of the section before they started working? Why hadn't he pulled his uncle under the canopy with him? The questions went on and on, and there were no good answers. And there was no one left to forgive him.

Will told McLennon that he had a wife and son down in the valley, but he hadn't seen them for two years. He just couldn't bring himself to face them, to face what he'd done. That's why he had been working at the college; that's why he was now working at the farm. He was in a kind of self-imposed exile. An exile that would never end.

McLennon listened as Will finished speaking. For a long time the two men just stared at each other. Then McLennon spoke.

"Do you believe in God?" he said.

"No, not really," Will said. "I guess I used to, but I just don't see the point anymore."

"Me either," McLennon said. "I guess that's why AA didn't take for me."

"I could see that," Will said.

"Thing is," McLennon said. "Who do you ask *for* forgiveness if you don't believe in God?"

"I don't know."

"Me either," McLennon said. And then, after a moment, he suggested matter-of-factly, "Maybe we could forgive each other."

"Yeah," Will said, laughing dismissively. "Maybe."

"I forgive you," McLennon said earnestly—so earnestly, the lights in the house seemed to dim momentarily. The world drained of color. Things seemed to be happening in slow motion.

"Dammit," Will said, his voice breaking. "I forgive you, too."

The color returned to the kitchen. Outside, night had fallen and a sense of peace descended upon the world. Will and McLennon decided to have a drink to celebrate their newfound power, then another one, and so on and so on until they were both drunk. They put on a movie and settled in for the night. First, it was *Unforgiven* starring Clint Eastwood. Then it was *The Outlaw Josey Wales*. By the time they got to *A Fistful of Dollars*, they were on the verge of passing out. Five minutes in, they were both asleep, sprawled out on the enormous sectional in front of McLennon's sixty-one inch high definition TV.

Will woke with a start at six the next morning. He was badly hungover, but his body was timed to the rhythm of the horses, so he got up and went outside and went about his chores. McLennon was still snoring on the couch when he left him, so he covered him with a blanket before going out.

He was moving slowly that morning, and it took him twice as long to finish his chores. When he returned to the main house around eleven o'clock, he found McLennon's body on the kitchen floor, cold and unresponsive. His kit was on the floor next to him, and it didn't take a coroner to figure out what had happened. One came anyway and pronounced him dead after Will called 911, and the cops and the ambulance came and went. He was the victim of a suspected overdose, a determination that was later confirmed by the toxicology report. The actor was gone.

* * *

Will stayed on for a few months after McLennon died to help Trevino sell off the horses and prepare the estate for sale. He finally called his wife, and they met for the first time in two years. They didn't get back together, but Will started to see his son regularly, and they developed a good relationship.

Will moved out to California where he worked as a horse trainer for film and television. His son came to visit him often, and they would ride out to a point overlooking the Pacific Ocean and watch the waves roll in, one after the other. The sea was a deep blue, painful to look at, like a bruise. The sky was a lighter blue that stretched on and on, far beyond what the eye could see. Against the blue rose the brown hills of southern California and a sense of endless possibility. Late at night, when his son was asleep, Will would watch McLennon's old films and confess his sins. There in the darkness, he could hear someone offer forgiveness.

The One Life We've Been Given

I don't like imagining my life (or Being) adding up
to a Nothing Burger. Yeah, with cheese of exotic origin
but still nothing. My life would make a pretty good movie.
Movies are what we have in the United States of America
to save us from some poverty of Spirit. They're designed,

movies, to deliver us for the cost of a ticket and popcorn.
In some, everyone dies (say, Tarantino's *The Hateful Eight*).
If drive-in Westerns are anything, they're threatening. A man
almost gets gelded—that may be another movie where the life
we've been given is a gift until it isn't. If I had to point to my

flaws, I couldn't. Self-awareness seems to run from hillbillies.
But if we met in a diner off I-70, you alone in a booth beside
a clock with Trump's wounding on its face, white blue red,
me slouching in a dead father's last full-length winter coat,
I hope you'd laugh at hearing that a film in which everyone

dies has that, at least, going for it. Might you be lonely and
hand me your number on a napkin of black-inked integers?
When I call, might I offer a Disney fairytale where Death
is reducible to the illumination in the eyes old yellering it
elsewhere (which is to say, anywhere) along these roads.

Three Chords and the Truth

scores every prep-kitchen morning with its nicked blade
of cornpone and twang, galloping from the cross-eyed
dishwasher's dusty radio like a posse of flint-skinned notes
tuned, just to pester, one hungover waitress, stuck

riding the steel guitar's syrupy notes long enough
to tar it all as *hillbilly bing-bang,* spit with all the muster
of a woman who's slept through her alarm,
punched in late and is now playing catch-up.

In a land of music, where a soaking stock pot bobs along
to a money beat, and the bubble dancer mouths every refrain
like a grievance, this day too will scale its way toward coda,
starting with the iceberg she'll core by bringing

each green head to the counter with a slam,
adding thunder to the roux of the time clock's dim tick.

The Harvest

Old hens and roosters wanted please
reads a handwritten sign near the till.
Cash only says another.

Ripe tomatoes and cucumbers and garlic
and squash survive July's heat on folding
tables. Watermelon and corn. Melons.

What I want, red potatoes for sale
by the quart, are sold out.
The boy behind the counter asks

in his Old Order elocution
if I mind waiting while more
are dug up—if I mind that they are dirty.

Do I mind dirty potatoes and getting
to watch his business partner,
also young, barefooted and wearing suspenders

over a stained white shirt,
pull a toy wagon over gravel
and grass and down a garden row

to stoop over and like a magician
draw from the ground a dozen
starchy spheres that I will wash

by hand and savor with boiled ears of corn?
Behind the farmstand, a young girl
hides from her older sister going about

her chores in the barn. Sneaks a vegetable
meant for sale from a crate and takes a bite.
Conceals it in her palm and pretends she's done

nothing wrong as she strides away,
her tastebuds and feet as well-acquainted
with this patch of earth as anyone.

Flies buzz. The hot sun shines down.
No, I do not mind. For this,
I've got nothing but time.

At a Certain Age

I'm warning you
don't go walking on the Sou'side
in the middle of a hot August Saturday.
Music blares out from the Tiki Lounge
          (its entrance, a huge wooden god's mouth).
          The music hums out of other joints.
You'll forget your grey curls,
forget your 60+ years—
you lived through the 60's
which became the 70's . . .

You start to cakewalk down the sidewalk.
Student types, 18- to 30-somethings, all around you,
sniggering at each other.   Or, you'll moonwalk, twirl,
and tap your heels. They look through you, talk to each other:
And she says I'm your worst woe or your two worst woes. (What?).
They wriggle in black-and-white dresses that fit like snake skin
on their curvy hips, or they prance in shorter-than-short skirts.
What are you two mumbling about back there, says one girl to the
     couple
behind her.   You're invisible.

You'll turn down 16th Street, head held high.
By the time you're past Muriel Street,
          it grows quiet. Franklin Court:
          brick row homes neat / matching
          you could live here in some fantasy.
Far enough from the flow, flow, flow of the heat
and chatter, far enough from the revving motorcycles

in impromptu parades, riders waving to the sidewalks.
     Keep walking to Merriman Court.
     Secluded oval street that turns back on itself.
     An island in the middle of sweet, little frame houses
for you and your bearded sweetie, or you & your female sig. other,
it's your flavor. You could hang out here, feel as if . . .
you were on vacation for at least a fortnight.

Apalachin Spring

Grackles made him apoplectic. A noisy, dark whirl of them descended upon Ernie's tidy feeding station, scattering sunflower seeds everywhere. He shoved the glass patio door aside and raced out, waving his arms.

"Get out of here, you grubby thieves! Scat!"

Filomena Mingarelli, just home from her dog grooming job, happened to glance out the kitchen window and saw her neighbor gesturing angrily and shrieking. The silver maple trees and forsythia shrubs dividing their property were just starting to bud, so she had an unfettered view of the spectacle. Ernie's voice was so loud it magnified the throbbing headache she had brought home from work, triggered by a deafening mix of hairdryers and high-pitched yipping.

She rubbed her brow and reached into the cupboard to get a cocktail glass. A large ice cube pinged the glass, followed by a few shakes of bitters, a solid pour of Kentucky bourbon, and a splash. Filomena twirled her finger in the glass before sipping.

Ahh. Medicine.

Her neighbor had retreated inside, so she donned a fleece jacket and went out back to sit on the patio chair and relax. The sun had already sunk behind the hilltop, lowering the temperature to forty-nine degrees. She didn't care. After the never-ending winter they'd just been through, it felt as warm as early summer.

Spring evenings calmed her. Filomena often sat outside for hours watching the color drain from the sky and violet dusk slowly cloak their hill. Usually, when Venus brightened straight ahead in the western sky, she knew it was time to go in. This time of year, the mosquitoes and gnats were still sleeping, so she could close her eyes and just focus on the melodious birdsong. She would hear the cheerful burbling of house finches and song sparrows first, followed by a Carolina wren duet—one on vocals, the other on percussion. Songs of robins and cardinals intertwined in the final chorus of the day, interspersed with a mourning dove's sigh.

Filomena sipped the amber drink, then pushed her shoulders back into the patio chair, stretched her legs straight out, and rotated her ankles. Standing all day on those hard floors wreaked havoc with her calf muscles and back. Today she groomed two goldendoodles, one Great Pyrenees, and five little stinkers. Exhausting! Her index finger still ached from the nip a Pomeranian gave her. Filomena let the bourbon's smoky fire numb the pain.

"I'm too old for this nonsense." She heaved a big sigh.

A clatter of wings circled above. The grackles swooped down to feed upon whatever they had missed on their first raid. Ernie must have been watching for their return.

"No. You. Don't!" He chased after them with the slotted metal spatula he'd been using to turn tilapia in a frying pan. "Go steal someone else's food!"

Filomena rubbed her brow as he kept screeching at the birds.

"Hey, Ern! Give it a rest, will ya?"

"I'll have you know I spent a fortune on those sunflower hearts."

She shrugged at him. "Everybody's gotta eat."

Ernie lowered his head and glared over his glasses.

"I see everybody's got to drink, too. Right, Fil?"

She squinted and muttered, "Stunad."

"Hope you're not becoming a drunk like your dad."

His words hit like a meaty punch to her gut. Filomena stood, grabbed her glass, and slammed the back door behind her. She plopped onto the oversized recliner in her living room, sputtering.

"All I wanted to do was relax after a long day of work. Is that too much to ask?" She raised her hands to the universe.

It didn't answer.

* * *

The grackles stuck to their feeding schedule, and every evening that week, she'd return home to Ernie squawking at them. She couldn't wait until foliage filled in the trees, providing a buffer for his antics.

Friday evening turned sunny and warm, so she brought a tall glass of ice water outside and a puzzle book.

After successfully chasing away another flock of grackles, Ernie sneered at her.

"Enjoying your vodka?"

"It's water, dumbass."

"Right. 'Water.'" Ernie made quotation marks in the air.

"What the hell's your problem?"

"Living next to a classless Ceccanesi."

He knew that would bug Filomena. Yes, her grandparents immigrated here from Ceccano, Italy, to work in the shoe factory at the bottom of the hill. So did many other families in this neighborhood. Her grandfather bragged that he and his coworkers sewed the boots worn by every member of the U.S. Army in World War I.

After high school, her father also joined the company and worked in the tannery until the accident that disabled him. He was lowering a huge cowhide into the tanning vat, slipped on the wet floor, and fell partially in. The chemicals burned his left arm so badly that he was never able to use it again. Young and married with a son and daughter, he had to depend on his wife working as the factory owner's housekeeper to pay their bills. It broke his pride.

She had grown up breathing the acrid black smoke that bellowed from that factory, and any time she got a whiff of something that smelled similar, she'd think of her poor dad and how unfair life could be.

Ernie's parents had immigrated here from Italy shortly after a liberal arts college opened blocks away from the shoe factory. His father was hired as the art history professor there. They left their home in Guardiagrele, Abruzzo, and bought a newly built house on the Northside that had been constructed by an Italian stone mason. He'd imported the terracotta tiles for the roof from Tuscany.

Elegance emanated from every corner of that yard. They installed a long pergola on the patio and planted grape vines to climb it. His father built a brick outdoor oven next to it. The perfectly groomed perennial beds around the perimeter of the yard were accented with imported

Carrara marble sculptures. A wrought-iron fence enclosed the front yard, cinched by a driveway gate adorned with a gilded family crest.

The neighbors laughed at the ostentatious homestead that looked so foreign in the working-class neighborhood. Some referred to Ernie's parents as the Duke and Duchess of the Northside. Their yard's elevation did afford them a spectacular view of the Susquehanna River below, and that probably reminded them of the lofty views from home.

A true sign of their wealth to Filomena was that Ernie's family dined on meat every night. Her family could just afford it on Sundays. Pasta beans—made with elbow macaroni, ceci beans, freshly grated Parmigiano Reggiano, and sauce—was a typical weeknight staple. Looking out the kitchen window as he ate his peasant food, her father had to stare at the opulence behind their standard-issue shoe company home. That's when he started visiting Nino's bar on the corner every afternoon.

It wasn't the fact that Ernie belonged to a higher social class that bugged Filomena. She groomed the dogs of many wealthy customers and had no issues interacting with them. It was the fact that he was a territorial, antisocial jerk.

Just ask the grackles.

"Classless? Ha! It's better than being a snooty Abruzese." She flicked her fingers from her chin at him and went back inside.

That night, as she scrolled down her Facebook feed, Filomena happened to come across a photo of an elderly woman in Maine who had a pet grackle. An amusing coincidence.

"Teddy so loves his cracked corn," the caption read.

A wicked idea came to mind.

What if I buy a bag of cracked corn and spread it on his lawn? Would that be too mean? They sure would enjoy their peasant food, though. Ha!

She knew by the routine of when his house grew dark that Ernie went to bed early. It would be possible to sneak into his backyard at night and spread cracked corn over the lawn. That is, if their neighbor's dog didn't see her.

* * *

Monday, on the way home from work, Filomena stopped at the feed store. She found the cracked corn in bins alongside peanuts, black oil sunflower seeds, and a seed mix specific to her area. She also saw those sunflower hearts. *They are pricey. Cracked corn is far cheaper.* Still, she filled a plastic bag with large scoops of it and secured it with a twist tie.

This will drive him insane, she thought, tossing it in her car trunk with a laugh.

After dinner, she went outside to the patio with a book—a murder mystery set in Catania, Sicily. As she read, laughter distracted her. She glanced up and saw Ernie giving a fancy blond woman a tour of his gardens. Her powdery sweet perfume was so strong she could smell its scent on the breeze. The woman had a little dog in her arms. Filomena sat up.

"Is that the nasty Pomeranian that bit me?" she whispered.

The woman holding the dog laughed at something Ernie said; the Pomeranian growled at him.

"No, Mia. Stop that. Mr. D'Alessandro is a nice man."

Mia, that's the little stinker's name. I hope she bites him, too.

Mia's owner had been apologetic about the nip she'd given Filomena. When the woman paid for the dog's grooming, she left her a hefty tip.

What's a nice woman like her doing with him? she wondered. Filomena leaned forward in her chair, straining to hear any bit of their conversation.

"Yes, this pergola would be a perfect setting for the tea party, Ernesto. I'll tell the opera guild's fundraising team to be in contact with you."

"It would be my supreme honor," he replied and then escorted the woman and dog to her car.

A tea party, huh. Opera guild? When will they hold it there? They'd probably have to wait until at least May when the weather is better. Maybe I should hold off on my cracked corn revenge until then.

* * *

Over the next few weeks, the weather behaved like a temperamental teenager. It swung from sunny moods to soaking rain to brief snow squalls spitting flakes and graupel that vanished as soon as the skies cleared.

Leaves on the backyard trees were on the verge of bursting through their buds—if only they'd get a couple of days of warmth in a row.

One Friday evening in mid-April, the temperature climbed to seventy-five degrees. Finally, she could go outside and read again. She tucked the book under her arm, grabbed a glass of red wine, and carried it outside with a plate of cheese, a few grapes, crackers, and peppered salami—what she called a "girly dinner" for when she was too tired to cook. The birds sang in full chorus around her. Heat radiating off the stucco walls of her house warmed her back. Small puffs of clouds drifted slowly in the turquoise dome overhead.

Suddenly, another racket.

"You damn birds! Get out of there! Go. GO!"

"Please, Ern. I'm trying to read here."

"Reading? What? Some dumb romance?"

"Actually, it's about a Sicilian woman who kills her neighbor for yelling too much." (Yes, she was exaggerating the plot.)

"Figures you'd read a novel about mobsters."

"What the hell is that supposed to mean?" She set the open book face down on her lap.

"C'mon. Everyone on the hill knows your dad was at that capo's house in Apalachin when it was raided."

Damn him. She didn't know how to respond. According to her mother, Filomena's father was there—*but only because he was helping the butcher make a large meat delivery,* she repeated to herself. The butcher felt sorry for Mr. Mingarelli's disability and would occasionally bring her father along on deliveries, paying him off the books. They had been to the house the day prior to drop off a large order. However, on the day of the raid, a large group from Detroit showed up unexpectedly, and the capo called the butcher at the last minute saying he needed more steaks—immediately. Just as they were backing out of the capo's driveway, the cops pulled up and blocked their exit. "Of course, he was innocent," her mother had said. Her father never spoke about it, and Filomena knew instinctively that it was not a subject to be discussed.

"He was helping the butcher make his delivery. That's all," Filomena now spoke.

"Oh, Mr. Stacconi?" Ernie replied. "You mean the guy who ordered the hit on the owner of the dry cleaners after he found out he'd had an affair with his wife? Butcher *indeed*. Your father kept great company."

"If you know so much local history, why don't you write a book?"

Zing! She smiled wryly.

That shut him up. Filomena knew that Ernie aspired to be a historian, but no academic press ever expressed interest in his writings. Unfortunately, he had not inherited a talent for writing from his father, who was a true scholar. Ernie gave up his dream and eventually found work teaching Italian at the local high school.

He spun around and marched back to his house. As soon as he slid his patio door shut, she took a sip of wine.

Finally, Filomena thought. She wrapped a piece of salami around a chunk of Asiago and ate it with relish.

Sitting there, Filomena thought about how similar their lives were, despite their difference in social class. Both had one sibling. Ernie's sister married a wealthy gallery owner in Manhattan and never looked back. Her brother lived in Raleigh, where he was transferred by the computer manufacturer that moved out of town. He rarely visited. When their parents died, both inherited the family home in a town that industry abandoned, draining away the last remnants of its wealth. Neither had married. Both had lived nearly seventy years without realizing their dreams. Filomena had been studying fashion design at a SUNY college until her mother was diagnosed with cervical cancer and she dropped out to care for her. Even though her mother eventually stabilized after treatment, Filomena never returned to finish her degree.

They each found contentment in the familiarity of surroundings that echoed their ancestral homeland. (Even the church and its tower looked like a view straight out of Ceccano.) The routine of their daily lives never faltered. Both knew there was no change ahead; this was the course they'd stay on until the end of their days.

A lone grackle with a shimmery blue head landed in the pear tree that her grandfather had planted behind the house. It puffed up and then emitted a metallic-sounding squawk. *Such beautiful birds they are,* she thought. *He should be grateful that they visit his yard.*

* * *

On the first Friday evening in May, she opened the car trunk at the grocery and found the cracked corn bag tucked in the back.

"Oops! I forgot about that. Better get it out of here," she said to no one in particular. She carried it inside and set it on the kitchen counter. Through the window, she noticed movement in Ernie's yard. Leaves almost fully blocked the view now, but she was able to make out Mia, the Pomeranian's owner, and two other women setting up card tables under the pergola. "Hmm, must be the tea party's tomorrow."

Someone knocked at the front door. Filomena's eyes widened when she opened it and saw Ernie standing there with a large pink hydrangea.

"I was at the nursery today buying perennials, and they had a buy two, get one free sale. Thought this would look nice on your patio wall next to your chair."

Her jaw gaped, but she couldn't speak. She was so stunned. In all the time they'd been neighbors, Ernie had never given her anything.

"What a nice surprise," she said finally as she accepted his gift. "It's beautiful." She leaned in to sniff it.

He rolled his eyes, laden with disdain.

"Hydrangeas don't have a scent."

"Oh," she laughed. "Do I leave it in this container, or should I plant it immediately?"

"If you have a nice urn, I'd put the container in that. If not, it will be fine for now in its pot. You can plant it in the fall."

"Well, this is certainly lovely, and I thank you. Are you having some sort of—" Filomena couldn't finish her question because he walked briskly away. She stood silently for a few seconds, confused by his gesture. "How weird. But good-weird. Am I on camera or something?" She stepped onto the porch and peeked around the arborvitae that hemmed it but didn't see him. Filomena stared at the heavy plant in her arms. "Huh. Very nice."

She carried the pot outside and set it down on the table before deciding on the right location. If she placed it on the small wall surrounding her patio as he'd suggested, next to her chair, then it might provide some privacy. She tested the view from the chair. *Perfect!*

Her eyes drifted up to the beautiful plant. The globe-shaped blossoms were the exact light pink hue of her house. *Boy, he's so good with details,* she thought. She wondered what had spurred his gift. Had he felt bad about the awful things he had said about her father? Was this the only way he could ask forgiveness?

The ladies from the opera guild were still working long after sunset. Filomena thought briefly about her plan to spread the cracked corn on his lawn after they left, but she'd had a change of heart. Ernie's surprising gesture touched her. It would be awful to respond to his spontaneous act of generosity with cracked corn cruelty. No, she would take the bag down to the park by the river and toss its contents to the ducks instead.

Filomena and Ernie had never gotten along when they were young. All the kids in the neighborhood gravitated naturally to her as their leader. It was probably because she had a big growth spurt at nine and towered above them all. She had also mastered an intimidating glare that ensured no one crossed her.

Just a year separated them, but everyone assumed Ernie was much younger. "Speak English," they'd taunt him when he slipped into his parents' native tongue. They mocked his beautiful home. "You think your poop doesn't stink!" He'd heard that insult more than once on the playground. Ernie withdrew from his peers. Filomena recalled that she never ran into him when they were in high school. She found that particularly odd because it wasn't a big school. *Where was he hiding?* she now wondered. *I should have been kinder to him back then,* she thought as she turned off the nightstand lamp. *Maybe he would have turned out happier and not become so mean.*

That night as she slept, a dark thought crossed her subconscious mind. It was so upsetting that it woke her with a gasp—

Wait a minute. Did he give me a plant that matches my house and tell me exactly where to place it so that it would camouflage me from his party guests?

"How dare he!" she hissed into the still night.

That was the end of her sleep. Though she stayed in bed until seven, her mind roiled with proper responses to his "gift." A plan emerged. She retrieved a pair of binoculars stored in the closet and set them on the kitchen counter. Then she texted two friends and invited them to come over for drinks later. She finished her shopping list and headed out.

Ernie's guests began arriving at a quarter to three that afternoon. As soon as she saw them gathering, Filomena fired up the backyard grill and then raised the umbrella over the patio table.

Next, she set out six skewers on a platter in the kitchen and began sliding chunks of lamb spiedies onto them. A local specialty she bought from Russo's Market at the corner, the meat was marinated with olive oil, red wine vinegar, lemon juice, garlic chunks, and chopped fresh herbs— oregano, parsley, and mint. There were plates and cutlery, napkins, a fresh-baked loaf of sliced Italian bread from the market, and wine glasses already arranged on one tray. Another tray had a "girly dinner" plate of salami, cheese, crackers, figs, and olives alongside a cookie plate of pizzelle, amaretti, and some chocolate-dipped biscotti. Once she was done preparing the skewers, she washed her hands and put foil over all the food before carrying everything out to the patio, including the binoculars.

She lifted the grill lid and set the skewers on top of the cooking grate. Before long, the spiedies' intoxicating aroma rose from the grill. Lucky for her, a breeze was flowing northward and carried the scent right into Ernie's yard. The tea party guests stared at the towers of egg salad and cucumber sandwiches in front of them as their stomachs noted something more enticing next door.

"Oh my *God!* Are you cooking lamb spiedies?" Filomena's friend yelled as she walked around the side of the house. She handed her a bottle of Montepulciano wine. "I haven't had them in years!"

"Remember the old men that used to grill them at that little stand outside the tannery," her other friend said as she placed a tossed salad and a platter of bruschetta with toasted bread rounds on the table. "That smell would rise through the Northside, and we'd all be begging our parents to go down and buy some."

"My pop said that he could buy three spiedies for a dollar when he was working on the avenue."

"That'd cost you five bucks today."

"Don't get me started on the *medigans* putting chicken spiedies in sub rolls," Filomena said to the others as she lowered the grill lid. "Am I right?"

"*So* right, Fil. The only way to do it is to wrap a single slice of Russo's bread around the chunks of lamb and slide them off the skewer."

"Who wants wine?"

Filomena raised her hand and then turned on the Bluetooth speaker next to the food.

"We need music." She searched for the Italian Dinner Party playlist on her phone and clicked on it. Louis Prima began singing his medley of "Just A Gigolo" and "I Ain't Got Nobody." She cranked the volume, and heads turned immediately from the tea party welcome speech toward her yard.

Her friends started singing along as she lifted the grill lid, and a puff of spiedie smoke rose.

"Are they done yet? I'm starving?"

Filomena grinned as she turned the metal skewers with a cooking mitt. "Just a minute more, I think."

"By the way, I love that hydrangea. Where'd you get it, Fil?"

She jabbed a mitted hand toward Ernie's house.

"Hey, he's got company over there. I didn't know he had any friends—thought he was a loner."

"They're from the opera company. He offered the use of his backyard for their tea party."

"Ooh, fancy."

She pointed at the binoculars. "Have a look."

Her friends took turns staring at Ernie's guests.

"They're *soooo* bougie."

"Did you see the one who looks like an 80-year-old Lady Gaga?"

Filomena laughed as she grabbed the binoculars. "You're right. Nice poker face there, lady."

"Those snobs think they're so classy eating that froufrou food."

"Yeah, but we've got the spiedies. C'mon, girl. Let's eat!"

After she carried the platter to the table, Filomena turned up the speaker's volume slightly. She knew that the more her friends drank, the louder they'd talk, trying to hear each other over the music.

"Ooh! I love this song," her friend yelled as Louis Prima started singing "Che La Luna." The three women clapped and sang along with him.

The head of the opera guild whispered to Ernie.

"That's quite some competition we have over there. Do you think they'd mind if you went over and asked them to turn down the music?"

Ernie reddened. He was furious at Filomena. She rarely entertained guests, especially such raucous ones. Why today?

"I can bring out a speaker and microphone."

"A polite request's not an option?"

Ernie closed his eyes and shook his head. "Not with her ilk. I'll be right back."

He got up from the head table and walked the length of the pergola to go inside. As he passed tables of guests, he noted many were discussing the appetizing scent of the spiedies. It angered him. The poor caterer had worked very hard to make an authentic British high tea presentation, and grilled peasant food was destroying the ambience.

Before the guests started on the sweets tier, the lead tenor and soprano of the opera company walked over to the music director who sat by an electronic keyboard. They would be singing the famous duet, "O Soave Fanciulla" from Puccini's *La Bohème*, the music director said. "We are proud to announce that we're bringing *Bohème* back to kick off this year's season." Guests applauded the news.

Downhill from them, Dean Martin began singing "That's Amore."

"Cher was freaking amazing in *Moonstruck*," Filomena's friend yelled.

"To Cher! Salute!" They clinked their wine glasses and stood, arms linked, swaying and singing along with Dean.

Under the pergola, an opera patron whispered to her husband, "I don't know which performance to watch."

"I think the food and drink's better over there," he responded with a nod toward Filomena's house.

The three women were still partying by the time the stars came out. Ernie's house had been dark for hours.

"Ugh, I gotta get up early tomorrow. Shall we go?" Filomena's friends nodded at each other.

"You okay to drive home?"

"Fil, we live four blocks away from you."

They laughed.

"Still, please text me when you both get home safely. People drive fast down these streets on Saturday nights."

"You sound like my mom, Fil."

"Hey, I care about you two. Okay?"

"Yes, Ma."

After they left, Filomena tidied the table and brought the dishes back inside. When she went out one last time to double-check that she'd turned off the grill's gas, a tree branch snapped. She froze, sensing someone was in her yard.

"Satisfied?"

"Ernie?"

"That was quite a spectacle you staged this afternoon." He walked toward her.

What the heck was he doing skulking about her yard at night? She wondered if there was a dark side to him she hadn't known about.

"We were celebrating the first beautiful weekend of the year. You got a problem with that?"

"Should I? Was it intentional?"

"Hmm, I dunno. Was bringing over a big ass hydrangea to camouflage me from your snooty guests intentional?"

He laughed. "Yes."

"Ha! I *knew* it."

She thought she smelled whiskey on his breath.

"Lamb spiedies were a brilliant choice. No escape from that scent. It carries for miles."

"Thank you. The prevailing breeze toward your house helped."

What does he want? she wondered. Filomena felt uneasy. *Is he angry enough to hurt me?*

"Do you know the history of the lamb spiedie?"

"Weren't there two brothers from Italy who started making them in their restaurants here?"

"Yes, that's true. But there's more to the story. Mind if I sit down?"

What was she going to say? She pointed at a chair. "Help yourself."

"Those brothers immigrated here from Abruzzo."

Here we go, she thought. *Lecture time.*

"The dish is called *spiducci* there. Exact same concept, similar recipe."

"Cool. I love cacio e pepe, and that comes from the Ceccano region."

He smiled strangely.

"True, but it doesn't have the cult-like following that spiedies do."

She was tired and wasn't in the mood to argue about the regional dishes of Italy.

"You know my father was there that day in Apalachin, too."

Filomena raised her eyebrows.

"Your dad was a mobster? I thought he taught art history."

"He did. You know, not everyone in the mob was running around rubbing people out like *The Sopranos*. One day, you might need a favor, and someone will give you assistance. It came with the caveat that another day would come when you had to return that favor, and you couldn't say no."

Filomena pulled out a chair and sat down. "I get it. Tell me what happened to your father."

"When they started the college, one of the local bosses needed to launder some money and thought that would be a good place to hide it. He was friends with a politician who was pushing the cause to open the college. This guy liked art and thought it should be taught there. He made a sizable endowment to start the art program there with the caveat that my father be hired to run it."

"Did he know your father?"

"No, but he was a fan of Caravaggio's paintings and had read my father's book about him."

"That's wild. Did your father know about the deal?"

Ernie sat back in his chair and laughed.

"My father had an enormous ego. The slightest flattery would get him to do anything for you. He thought the college sought him out because of his renown. He told everyone in Guardiagrele that a prestigious American university had hired him."

She laughed.

"When did he find out the truth?"

"The day of the raid—he'd been summoned there to appraise the value of a painting as a favor to the boss who'd made that endowment. The rest of the guests were enjoying the barbecue outside as my father was led to a darkened room within the house. When the boss unveiled the painting, my father recognized it immediately as a painting that had been stolen recently from a museum in Tuscany. He tried not to show the outrage he felt when the boss asked its value, then in the same breath delivered the news to him about how he'd been hired for the college."

"That must have devastated your father."

"It did. There were two other occasions where he was summoned out of the blue to appraise works. Both were stolen works of Italian painters."

"An offer he couldn't refuse, eh? Well, at least your father didn't take part in the theft."

"True, but as he was leaving the capo's house before the raid happened, he ran into your father. Their eyes met, but they didn't say a word to each other. He felt disgraced to be seen there, especially by his neighbor."

"Man. What were the odds of that happening?"

"Around here?" Ernie gestured with his hands as he looked right, then left. They laughed.

"My father never spoke about that day. Your dad's secret was safe with him."

"I'll have you know my father always spoke highly of your father. Said that despite his injury and subsequent depression, he was an honorable man."

"That's a very kind thing to say. Thank you, Ernie."

He nodded, then folded his hands on the table and leaned toward her.

"Fil, if you don't mind—I have a special favor to ask."

"Oh, you can have the hydrangea back. That's okay."

"No, that's not it."

"What then?"

"My windows were open all day, and the scent of your lamb spiedies permeated my house. Do you have any more of them?"

"Yes, why?"

"Would you grill some for me?"

"Now?"

"I'm starving. I'll be thinking of them all night if I don't eat some and won't be able to sleep. It's all I can smell."

She laughed out loud.

"You're a piece of work, Ernie. Hey, why not? I'll cook you some but only if you promise to do *me* one favor."

"Sure. Anything. What is it?"

"Be kind to those damn grackles."

He smiled. "You're right, Fil. Everybody's gotta eat."

Kids

Casings clink on the gravel drive and my brother sets his feet so as not to flinch. His shoulder bruises with ripe plums, recoil kickback into baby fat. He hates these lessons, the gunsmoke in his blond, the grease red beneath his fingernails. I like to rest my cheek on the vinyl siding of the house and feel the ricochet shiver through my jaw. I like how the bang peels away from its other sounds: sigh of safety released, hairpin lurch of trigger, the woods an aria of echoes. I do not plug my ears, and sound tears. At dinner we eat meat and do not set a place for the paper target tacked to the tree. Its holes are mouth, eyes, heart like swiss cheese, pale and sexless in the mottled moonlight. My stomach bloats. When August peels in the heat and the schoolhouse doors tear open, my brother and I will not scream at the gunshots. Just a neighboring farmer popping groundhogs. Heads like bags of paint. I lay in the grass and tear the browned shoots by the roots. In my right ear, tinnitus the cry of kits without their mother, or maybe the other way around.

Morning Star

above blue-black trees—
Satellite? or one of God's tiny eyes?
A pickup winds through woods with warm-throated motor,
one headlight then two breaking a prism refracted in rising fog
beyond my bedroom window. Its diesel curls along the riverbank
where yesterday I saw a buck . . . then truck is gone

and yard and sky fall to indigo again.

I pull the quilt up and hope the furnace will kick on;
remember Grandpa's boots like clockwork at the homeplace:
off to the factory, Stanley Thermos & lunchbox in hand,
slow gravel dutiful under his tires,
crossing the Cuyahoga,
waiting for dawn.

Embarrassing Notes From an Appalachian Adolescence

For a writer, embarrassment is a theme equally valid as triumph or success. But "embarrass" seems a word in transition, evolving on its own. Webster's Ninth New Collegiate Dictionary (1987) defines "embarrass" in several ways, none of which quite conveys what we feel in that compromising moment. My word processor's electronic thesaurus gets closer to current usage. Its top three choices are humiliate, mortify, and shame—all bullseyes on that gut-pit implosion we feel when embarrassment strikes . . .

Overpowered at the Bee

My earliest formal education occurred at Mt. Braddock Public School, named for British General Edward Braddock, whose path to disaster on the Monongahela River outside what's now Pittsburgh, early in the French and Indian War, passed, literally, beneath our recently condemned but still occupied schoolhouse. When I reached the sixth grade, my mother transferred my sister Kim and I to St. Aloysius Catholic school, about four miles away in the borough of Dunbar, named for another British officer in that same catastrophic campaign. While enrolled at Mt. Braddock, we crossed a sheep pasture, angled downhill through woods, then crossed Gist Run to reach school. Frontiersman and local settler Christopher Gist was George Washington's guide on Washington's 1753 mission to warn the French to vacate western Pennsylvania. It wasn't obvious to us, but we'd walked to school every day through one of the most significant locations in American history.

Our transfer to St. Aloysius required automotive transport. Back then, public school buses didn't carry kids to parochial schools. We had a '55 "Shivy" for our family car, but our mother didn't yet drive, and Dad worked every day. Together with a couple of other mothers who'd made the same school switch, Mom arranged for a local James Dean-inspired and otherwise unoccupied youth to drive us to class and back. Those mothers never knew that for their few dollars paid our driver, our ostensibly bland school trips thrilled us with 100-mph vaults across railroad tracks, a brake- scorching, tire-squealing cow strike, at least one high-speed engine fire, and we kids' opening boxes of church envelopes the priest had instructed us to deliver home, then delighting in those pink packets swirling out the windows at 90 mph as unholy litter along the Mt. Braddock-Dunbar Road.

I attended St. Aloysius for only two years, but an observant nun noticed I could spell. So, in my seventh-grade term, our faculty of four sisters and one priest (he never learned what happened to those envelopes) chose me to represent St. Aloysius in the annual Diocese of Greensburg Spelling Bee.

These were august affairs for that time and place. Proud parents jammed into rows of seats, tight to the front, in a cavernous auditorium at St. Vincent's College, Latrobe. Sisters in black-and-white habits filed up and down the aisles as ushers, and two dozen nervous kids faced the expectant crowd from a row of folding chairs on the stage. Midway across the stage stood a plain lectern, topped with a microphone adjusted to accommodate middle-school height. At one corner of that stage, presiding from an elevated pedestal, sat The Monsignor, the highest priest in diocesan education.

Spelling bees worked this way. Chosen students took turns at the microphone, one speller at a time, while from his platform, Monsignor announced the word to be spelled by each. When a speller received his or her word, they were to pronounce that word into the mic, spell it, then pronounce it again, so that everyone in the auditorium knew the speller understood precisely what was expected. If you spelled your word correctly, you reclaimed your seat on stage and continued. A misspelled word wrought dismissal from the contest, and you were asked to take a seat among the spectators.

As the bee progressed, I retained my perch on stage through several rounds. Your turn comes quickly, though, as more misspellers are banished. With only four or five contestants surviving, I strode to the lectern to pronounce, spell, and pronounce my next assigned word.

"Benjamin," Monsignor proclaimed, "Your word is PARASOL."

A parasol, of course, is a flimsy umbrella, used as sun protection. I had never seen one. But I had grown up around hard-crusted, calloused, and sun-leathered mountaineers who assembled out of the hills every morning to work in my grandfather's small asphalt paving business through 90-degree days on 300-degree blacktop, and who ran their hill farms and logging operations on the side. Such men employ a chore-focused vocabulary, pronounced as it was learned from peers.

Surprised to be assigned such a softball word, I leaned into the mike, pronounced my word with confidence, then spelled out: "P, O, W, E, R, S, A, W." Sensing victory now, I pronounced it again. Before I even finished, suppressed giggles bubbled around the hall, here and there, the way the first kernels of popcorn burst at random in an oiled pot.

"Benjamin, that is incorrect. Leave the stage!" Monsignor commanded.

Baffled, I stood there with an expression that must have conveyed the incredulity of our modern-day "What?" when it's ejaculated with hunched shoulders and upturned hands.

"Please, Benjamin. Leave the stage," Monsignor repeated.

In seventh grade, in Catholic school, you do not disregard the Monsignor. I shuffled off stage, confused. A young nun referee, her black folds flowing, loped up the aisle to my side. Barely able to suppress her own chuckle, she opened a dictionary and tapped a long white finger on the entry—"parasol: a lightweight umbrella used as a sunshade, esp. by women."

A linguist trained in regional dialects could have explained why I'd heard, pronounced, spelled, and pronounced yet again, "POWERSAW," in response to an educated and traveled clergyman's spoken "PARASOL." Such enlightenment, though, could not have salved the embarrassment that darkened naïve defeat.

The Last Barrel Race

Like many rural Appalachians, I benefited in my youth from access to generational land. My grandfather had a small farm at the foot of the mountain, and my late grandmother's (his wife) people had a smaller, steeper farm near the crest. These tracts were three miles and about 1,500 feet in elevation apart. "Pap" still ran white-face Hereford cattle then. In summer, he grazed them on the slopes of his in-laws' mountain place, with its log barn and chestnut stake-and-rider fences. In winter, he herded those steers, a couple at a time, through a chute into a stake-bed truck and hauled them down to the lowlands where snow was less persistent. There, he fed them on hay we'd baled on the fields, then hauled them back up the mountain in spring. Back then, the two parcels' climates were distinct enough to make the seasonal moves worthwhile to him, even though he'd lost an eye, horn-gored, loading steers in his youth, and wore an ill-positioned prosthetic eye through those few years our lives overlapped.

My parents, sisters, and I lived about halfway between the two farms, so each was handy to reach on foot, by car, or on horseback, that latter form of travel common for us after my sister Kim's passion for horses bloomed, and she kept a horse or two fenced on Pap's lowland pasture.

Kim was a natural horsewoman and achieved regional fame for her dominance in "western games," rodeo events that demand riding skill and a fast, nimble, well-practiced mount. The most popular "western games" were keyhole and barrel racing, and my sister excelled at both, earning trophies and ribbons that festooned Pap's barn.

Barrel racing was her favorite event, where she rode her little quarter horse, "Chocolate." It's a timed competition, in which horse-and-rider pairs run the course in turn. Contestants enter the arena at an all-out gallop, crossing a starting line where the judge activates a stopwatch. Riders continue around a cloverleaf course of three steel barrels arranged like the bases on a baseball diamond. Their goal is to circle each barrel as fast and tight as possible, without tipping the barrel, then streak back across the finish. Fastest time wins.

Grange, 4H, and local saddle clubs held "horse shows" around the region in modest little plots and parks. These were like community rodeos in the West, though generally without "bucking" events.

But the biggest, most awaited horse show around was that held every summer in the arena at the Fayette County Fair. That arena was big-time. Bleachers marched skyward from a vast red dirt rectangle, bristling with light trusses for nighttime spectacles. Every kind of attraction, from a circus to demolition derbies, professional wrestling, and horse shows/rodeos, packed the locals under those lights.

Competition didn't attract me. I liked trail rides, informal sojourns through woods and across streams on looping routes around the mountains. On trail rides, we sometimes saw bears or rattlesnakes and always flushed deer. But a random event side-tracked my distaste for competition. A guy who owed my dad a hundred dollars finally squared his debt—with a horse.

The horse was a tall, lean pinto gelding, liver-and-white, its dark tones splotched wildly across alabaster flanks, face, and neck. He was nervous, headstrong, and initially difficult to saddle and ride, but his looks were stunning. To me, he came straight out of those revisionist western movies of the late 1960s, films like Little Big Man, A Man Called Horse, and Soldier Blue, which tried to reverse decades of degrading cinematic portrayals of Native Americans. In these later films, noble Indians mastered the plains, hunting buffalo and battling U.S. cavalry on pinto horses, as they indeed had done in history.

I'd seen them all, enthralled, and I saw the horse that settled my dad's debt as a way to live them. In my defense, such romantic fantasy was understandable for a teen of that time and place. Horsemanship, mounted or driven, is deep-rooted in Appalachian life, and we still lament the devastation of indigenous cultures of the Appalachian region, whose passing was bad enough in its own right, and with much to teach we who would inhabit these hills after.

But in decidedly un-Appalachian fashion, I named that horse Comanche, for the dominant equestrian culture of the Southern Plains. He chafed at a saddle, so I rode him bareback, which is not as difficult as it sounds if you synchronize your posture and muscular response to the horse's gait. He was fast, responsive, and agile, and his quick pivots prompted the unthinkable but burgeoning hope that I could beat Kim's time in the barrel race.

I set up a course in the pasture with empty asphalt-sealer barrels from Pap's work shed, placed at the specified 110-foot spans and ran Comanche through the cloverleaf only in Kim's absence. I wanted my victory to come as a surprise.

Comanche seemed born for the barrels. I didn't have a stopwatch, but our times felt good. To compete, though, he would need to accept the saddle. Nobody rides the barrel race bareback, and a saddle does offer an advantage. It enables the rider to lean harder into the turn around the drum, helping the horse pivot by shifting body weight to the rider's inward foot, supported by the stirrup.

Surprisingly, in a few sessions, that horse surrendered his disdain for being saddled. He enjoyed racing around tar-smudged barrels so much that he tolerated the additional weight cinched around his chest. I knew the people who ran the county fair horse show, so I registered for the barrel race, unknown to my sister, the local star of that event.

But I could not just do this in the conventional way. I had those noble Great Plains buffalo hunters to emulate, and I now had the pinto horse to make an impression. Those films I'd watched featured aspects of Great Plains horse culture that were easy to copy. Plains warriors and hunters decorated their horses with symbols that signified esteemed traits and deeds. Lightning bolts painted on the horse's legs summoned speed. A circle inscribed in paint around its eye enabled the mount to see an enemy and evade attack. Most compelling, a handprint painted on the haunch meant the rider had been wounded in battle. I concede that I could not have known or appreciated the authentic import of these symbols to the people who first invoked them, but at that time, from books and cinema, these were the interpretations I understood and imitated. And on the day of the barrel race, I painted all these same symbols on Comanche's splotchy hide. He looked like he had galloped off the plains from a hundred years in the past.

My dubious preparations didn't stop there. Modern competitive barrel racing specifies an official dress code. It mandates a collared, long-sleeved, western shirt, traditional cowboy boots, and a classic cowboy Stetson. I don't know if that code was in force 60 years ago at the Fayette County Fair, but all other riders complied with a mutually understood standard. Still, nobody contested my dress when I signed in at the arena. I wore knee-high, fringed, buckskin moccasins, advertised in Outdoor Life magazine for 19 dollars. Those mocs, along with a Puma Bowie hunting knife, were the first things I'd ever bought for myself with money earned shoveling asphalt on my summer job for Pap's paving company. Complementing the moccasins were a fringed leather sleeveless vest and a headband that trailed, Apache-style, in the mane of hair I'd managed to grow despite tense confrontations with my father.

For us, hauling horses to the fairground in a trailer wasn't necessary. Pap's farm was near enough for us to ride there, out one gate, then flanking Rte. 119 through what was then a Christmas tree farm but is now the site of a Rural King store and the declining Laurel Mall. At a walk, a horse and rider could reach the arena in half an hour. Kim had ridden over earlier in the day to socialize with her "horse people" friends and to compete in other events. I waited until early evening to saddle Comanche and ride over for the barrel race that night.

When we paced up through the contestants' gate, the fairground was all commotion and tumult. Calliope notes piped out over a midway swelling with gawking strollers, and spotlight beams waved and intersected on the purple sky. The smell of frying peppers and onions entwined with the warm scent of the livestock barns. When onlookers caught sight of my painted "war horse" and pressed in to ogle and stroke him, Comanche balked and sidestepped, his eyes wide in alarm. All the way across the grounds to the arena, curious patrons turned toward the fringed rider on a painted mount, gesturing for others to witness such a strange, atypical pair.

For the first time, doubt clouded my hopes for the race. Comanche had breezed through practice sessions, accepting a saddle for the joy of headlong gallops and tight pivots. Never had he shirked or faltered. But we'd always practiced alone, on a secluded pasture in afternoon sun. The fair, with its bustle, noise, and garish lights, was nothing like that serene setting. How would this inherently nervous horse perform in such an alien place? But he seemed to settle as we left the throng and trotted into the entrants' waiting zone at the arena's west end. Kim and Chocolate had already run the course, so my surprise appearance and expected triumph were still intact.

As your turn approaches in western game competitions, you guide your horse out of the common waiting area into a kind of "on-deck" chamber. This temporarily quiet vestibule is shielded from the view of spectators behind a gate that flings open as the timekeeper summons you to compete. There, awaiting the signal, riders goad their mounts to coil and tense for the imminent launch. Comanche was easily coiled. At the nudge of my heels, he sensed a sprint beyond the gate. Against a tight rein, there in quiet shadows, he pranced and reared, eager to attack the course.

A bull-horned voice exclaimed, "Go!," the gate flung open, and the Stetsoned timekeeper appeared, poised over the starting line, stopwatch at ready.

I loosed the reins, dug my heels into Comanche's flanks, and "clucked" my tongue. Then it was all horse. His whole mass dipped low as his legs gathered beneath him, then erupted. We shot out of that gate, throwing up clods from Comanche's hooves, into the arena and across the line. I felt nothing but speed and the powerful grace of equine stride.

Then we hit the lights—the glaring stadium orbs that illuminated two thousand faces, every one roaring out a clamor of cheering or jeering for a long-haired kid dressed in Indian caricature on a streaking painted pinto.

Comanche never slowed his breakneck pace. He just planted his steel shoes and stopped dead under the glare, like he'd hit a wall of light and noise. As rider, of course, I maintained all the momentum my mass and his velocity had built up through our initial streak. When Comanche stopped, I kept hurtling toward that first barrel, vaulting out of the saddle and over his head, flipping end-over-end into the arena's red dust, beneath all those bright lights, before those incredulous faces.

The crowd exploded. Their guffaws, backslaps, and pointing were too much to bear. A more composed cowboy might have remounted there in the crowd's reproach and continued the race. I did remount but could not command such courage. I turned Comanche back toward the gate, galloped out of the arena, and into the night. It was a long, dark, mortified ride back to Pap's barn.

Remembering the gut-pit implosion that burned in my core, I must have looked for some way to hide out forever in the pine tree maze. If I said anything to Comanche, it would have been, "That disaster was all my fault."

Kim, leaning on a front-row rail, had been among the astonished onlookers. Afterward, she shared words on my performance. None were consoling.

Lunchroom, First Day

Chronologically, this was the first of three youthful embarrassments. I present it here last because of its nature, mindful that others, in their adolescence, have been subjected to related but truly harmful experiences in schools, churches, or at home, from which they suffered real trauma.

My mother had her reasons for switching our school, most of them valid. Later, I often assured her of that from an adult perspective. One motivation, I'm sure, was religious immersion. My mother's family were Hungarian Catholics, not a worldview likely to be nurtured at Mt. Braddock Elementary.

To her credit, she wished us exposure to pious striving, possibly even chastely pious, since my younger sister was also subject to the switch.

The St. Aloysius "campus" of red brick church and school, shingled rectory, convent, and clapboard social "hall," clung to a hillside above the confluence of Gist Run and Dunbar Creek, overlooking the Western Maryland railroad tracks and Pechin Market and Café, home of the nationally famed ten-cent hamburger as extolled in the Wall Street Journal. Stone walls arrested the slope, impounding the leaning structures in place. Though any new school is menacing to an 11-year-old, I eventually harbored affection for St. Aloysius and still do. But events of my first sixth-grade day proved ironic, considering my mother's hope of piety.

Students ate their lunches, packed from home, in the social hall, a squat one-story rectangle set just outside the cluster of other buildings. On that first day, I must have been detained before lunch by some inductive procedure because I finished my lunch in the hall alone, after all other students had piled outside for noon recess.

A side door creaked open, and a slice of sunlight pierced the hall's gloom. Three older girls—eighth grade, the school's highest level—crept inside, closing the door behind them. Two, both brunettes, were tall and willowy. The third girl was blonde and petite. The girls glanced around, then slunk toward me, coiling around the bench where I ate. One of the tall pair did the talking.

"We bet you have a big brother at home," she purred, fingering my hair above an ear.

I did not, but muted by the situation's murky strangeness, could summon no response.

I stared into my chipped ham sandwich as the trio dropped their skirts and pulled off their panties.

Two sat, flanking me on the bench, while the third sat on the table before me, facing away but looking over her shoulder to continue the taunt. I felt paralyzed by a fear of turning my gaze in any direction.

"Bring your big brother around sometime," she said. "We'd like to meet him."

I can recall no further details about the encounter, except that no contact occurred beyond a girl's finger in my hair. I can't remember the girls getting dressed, how or when they left the hall—only that at some point I was alone again.

Amusingly, perhaps, I did, years later, try to rekindle a spark with two of the girls. But they undoubtedly harbored their own embarrassment from that incident, and we were older, so that their two-year seniority had expanded the adolescent, boy-girl, maturity gap between us, and I could never resurrect their interest. Eventually, I resigned their advances, not to any attraction to me personally, but simply to the allure of the new kid, a rarity in that little school. It had been a fleeting, anomalous event in an otherwise supportive place, yet one that still evokes some wistful speculations.

The Revolution (a Wurster poem)

When those four students were killed at Kent State
I thought this is it, the beginning.

I went over to CMU campus and saw them
throwing frisbees, reading and smooching under the trees.

That's when I knew
there would be no revolution.

Aquifer

An aquifer is the technical name,
the scientific one, for the mad tumult
and deluge of churning damp rocks
carried by once icy glacial water long made
tepid that flows, kind of, thirty feet beneath.

I prefer to call it what it's always been,
Pittsburgh's mysterious "Fourth River,"
what I still envision as an antediluvian
passage underneath the Golden Triangle,
a stalactite and stalagmite covered cavern
through which slinking in the parentheses
shaped emptiness is an Amazonian
waterway, filled with blind albino crocodiles
and bats the size of flying dogs,
of sauropod monstrosities with their long necks
and tyrannical lizards holding dominion even today.

But deep down enough all there is just their
bones fossilized to anthracite, any *elan
vital* left waiting to be immolated, their
spirits exorcized and powering
the downtown air conditioners
through which the cooling
aquifer now flows.

Rivers & Whistles

We were eating dinner at a tiny bar/restaurant in Pittsburgh's Homestead neighborhood when a train came barreling past the window. It rattled the bottles on the shelves and zoomed past the windows, making it impossible to read the graffiti on the railcars. Its whistle echoed through the valley, drowning out the hockey game on TV and the talk of other patrons.

My husband commented to the waitress about how close the tracks were, how strong the vibrations. "Any bottles ever break?"

She shrugged as she collected our empty craft beers. "Sometimes. The best part is when people from out of town run over to the windows like little kids."

"Really?" I raised my eyebrows.

"Really," she affirmed.

My husband and I exchanged amused glances. What was an everyday occurrence in Western Pennsylvania was apparently a bizarre, half-assed tourist attraction for out-of-towners.

That night, when we went to bed in our seventy-year-old brick home perched atop a hill that overlooked the former site of one of the largest steel mills, I thought about what the waitress had said about the visitors and those trains. Funny that something I heard daily rendered others wide-eyed and speechless. I fluffed my pillows and smiled when I realized I'd been hearing those trains and their low, echoey whistles for as long as I could remember.

They chugged along the Monongahela River and lulled me to sleep at the very first home I lived in—the same row house in Pittsburgh's historic South Side where my dad had grown up. A neighborhood packed with uneven brick sidewalks, a playground behind the library. The famous Pretzel Shop, still churning out handmade dough and treats. Mike and Tony's, where I'd go with my dad to get gyros and watch him play pinball in the shadow of neon lights. Streets lined with parking meters that I stood on tiptoes to push quarters into when I had the privilege of running errands with my mom. Trains were always in the background of the landscape.

When we moved a dozen miles to the suburbs, a little further along the same river, I could still hear those trains clanging along the rails past the site of the mills that were being razed to make room for retailers and restaurant chains. Without the city streetlights, it was so much darker at night in the new house, and at nine years old, it was unnerving. The one thing that helped me adjust was listening to those train whistles as I fell asleep. They accompanied me as I grew up, too—summers swimming in our inground pool, pop tunes blaring as I plastered boy band posters on my bedroom walls, sleepovers where I giggled with friends into all hours of the night, and scribbled the names of our crushes on the door of the cupboard below the stairs.

If there was ever a house to eclipse the ubiquitous train whistles, it was a house like Gram and Pap's. A bigger house, deeper in the suburbs, even further down the old Monongahela. I never realized how much I treasured the place until Gram put it on the market. It was two years after Pappy died, and much like I couldn't imagine living in a house with no train whistles in the background, I couldn't imagine life without the sanctuary that was Gram and Pap's.

The sprawling lawn, the "Pittsburgh potty" in the basement. The fireplace, complete with cast iron poker and skillet, and the bar with its mirrored walls from the seventies. The living room picture window that let in endless rays of sunshine in the summer and displayed the Christmas tree each year. The reassuring orangey glow from the streetlights shining through the sheer curtains when my sister and I camped out in their living room. The towering hemlock tree that provided shade to the hammock, swinging from creaking wooden pillars Pap had built and secured in small pools of concrete, with handprints, names, and dates scrawled by me and my cousins decades ago. The covered back porch, with its Astro-turf pad and vinyl awnings, sheltered us from thunderstorms— grandkids covering their ears and staring wide-eyed, wondering if the stories they heard about angels bowling were true. The squeaky metal glider, the picnic table where we ate birthday cake and Memorial Day burgers and opened bridal shower gifts and played Scrabble. Picking little brown pears from the tree in the front yard, popping popcorn over in the fireplace in the heavy cast iron skillet. Dial soap in the bathroom, sawdust in Pappy's creepy workshop at the bottom of the stairs, Elizabeth Taylor's White Diamonds perfume in Gram's bedroom.

And train whistles, always in the background. Rail cars carrying who knows what from one place to another, barreling down the same tracks as they had been for decades. Despite all the other changes in the world and my life, no matter how many times I moved, those trains and their whistles still somehow managed to permeate the landscape, much like the grit, the iron, and ore that seeped into Pittsburghers' blood, our subconscious.

The last time I visited my grandma, I memorized every corner of that house—every brick, every window, every cabinet. I breathed in the scent that stirs some of my best memories. I did my best not to cry and somehow muddled through the next few years, missing that house, my grandparents, my childhood.

Time, of course, helped, as did meeting my husband, getting engaged, planning a wedding, and buying a house of our own. A starter home, a bit of a fixer-upper, with original hardwood floors, antique glass doorknobs, a convenient laundry chute, and a friendly ghost. The old-fashioned light fixtures, the stark white tile in the bathroom, the god-awful curtains from the seventies. As we worked to make the house our own, painting and planting, remodeling and refreshing, the ever-present whistles echoed in the background. In some small way, that blaring, almost eerie cry helped me feel connected to my past.

Eight years after we closed on our first place and eighteen years after Gram sold her house, my husband and I found ourselves looking for a new home. We wanted more space, more quiet. I fantasized about Gram's house going on the market and buying it, coming full circle. But the same people who had moved into the house years ago must have been content, because no listing ever appeared on the real estate websites, and no sign ever graced the front yard.

We toured half a dozen homes and placed offers on several. Each time, we were crushed when we lost out to house flippers or buyers with bigger budgets. Frustrated by the ruthless selling market of 2021, we became so disenchanted that we decided to take a break. And then, only a few weeks later, we went to see the house on Inglewood.

It was the picture window in the living room that did it. Just like Gram and Pap's, it looked out over an expansive backyard that hosted clusters of trees, plenty of room for a pool, a garden, a fire pit, and a hammock. There were creatures too—deer and groundhogs, a pair of squirrels, a variety of birds, and even the occasional garter snake.

In spring and summer, the breeze frequently delivers the mingled scents of honeysuckle and lilac. The branches of a massive hemlock tree in a neighbor's yard reach over our fence.

There's a large bar in the basement, thankfully without seventies gilded mirrors. Three bedrooms, hardwood floors, and an upstairs bathroom that I'm pretty sure still has the same fixtures as my grandparents' house did in the sixties. An Astro-turf-covered porch, in a less garish color than the green at Gram and Pap's. An awning that allows us to sit outside and listen to the rain. A quiet street, a place for a family to grow, a place for memories to be made.

A dream I didn't realize I'd been waiting decades to recreate. One that I still can't quite believe came true.

And even though our new house sits on a hill overlooking the Youghiogheny River instead of the Monongahela, there are still trains chugging away in the valley, blasting their whistles into the air, reminding me that there are different ways to come full circle. Different ways to feel at home.

Drink Up

A black pump pushes pure
water at a cranked pace
—spits it in spurts
like what happens when
an artery is torn in two
yet this echoes a creaking rhythm
on rural farms everywhere

especially here in southeastern Ohio
water from a spring
is clear juice
with century old travel
through undeveloped land
scooped no doubt by hands of
wanderers or hunters or settlers

may taste a bit different now
pollutants making it tastier
while preserving the tiniest bits of life
for my gut to enjoy

And yet
this land I have
has been repurposed
from once ancient farming
to tree growth for pilfering a century ago
now into my hands that will cherish it
with a constant caressing of fur on feral cats
or a listen to singing tongues of migratory birds

or a sight of deer eating flowers
or a walk down a cleared game trail
to the ravine
at Ponder Point

I am repurposed here too.

Rural Pennsylvania!

Narrow dirt road
threading through forests
and fields—
no one could live so far
out in the country,
but look: there's a mailbox
among the weeds
and wildflowers
by the side of the road.

Antlers

Carl's petite hands shook as he pressed the cold steel of the Winchester 30-30 against his right cheek. He had never shot an animal as big as a deer before. He popped a couple rabbits with his 22 and shot a ruffed grouse and a gray squirrel with a BB gun, but a rifle and a deer were completely different. The gun was his grandfather's, and the young buck was bigger than Carl, with more testosterone pumping through its three-year-old veins than the twelve-year-old boy had in his entire body.

Carl couldn't count the number of points on the antlers. He figured it had six or eight. He kept losing sight of the animal as it wove between the mountain laurel and oak, following a small herd of does looking for acorns and lichen under the snow. Trying to line up the open sites on the beast's neck, Carl felt his heart beat faster, and his glasses fogged from holding his breath. He cursed his nearsightedness, wishing his eyesight were half as sharp as his brother Len's.

This was their first hunting trip together since Len's return from the war, and Carl's first official deer hunt since he came of age back in August. Carl's father was so proud that his youngest boy would finally join the family at deer camp that winter. And the fact that Len had come back alive and could join them made Carl's father even happier. Carl thought of how proud his dad and older brother would be if his first deer were a big buck. He pictured drinking corn whiskey around the table at camp with the rest of the men, toasting to the trophy kill that Carl imagined making.

But first, Carl had to kill the deer to make those dreams happen. His hands began to shake again as he looked through the gun sites. All he could see were the dark green leaves of the laurel. Scanning the forest, Carl's eyes fell upon the red brown fur of his prey; reacting instantly, he quickly pulled the trigger. Carl flew back with the gun's recoil, hitting his head on a large beech tree behind him.

He felt as if his head exploded. Was the buck dead? Had he even hit it? Should he wait or go look? Surely his dad and brother heard the shot. Carl knew he shouldn't go into the thicket too soon and scare a wounded animal. He had to sit tight for five or ten minutes and wait for the deer to die.

Len's voice broke the silence from behind, startling Carl. "Hey, little fella, was that your gun that went off?"

Carl said, "Sure was. My first buck. I think it's a big one." Pointing at the canvas bag his brother was carrying, he asked, "You get one, too?"

"Yup. Got the liver and heart in here for Ma. We were loading it into the truck when Pop and I heard you shoot. He's waiting back in the truck."

"Can we go find my deer now?" asked Carl with newfound excitement.

Len didn't answer, only walked toward the thicket of mountain laurel, motioning to Carl to follow slowly and step where he stepped.

Carl did see the motionless animal first, or his brother allowed him to think that. Carl immediately ran past Len, eager to get to his first deer and feel the pride of the kill. Kneeling, Carl lifted the animal's head to count the points on the antlers.

It was a doe. A big fat doe. Carl's first deer kill on the opening day of buck season was an illegal doe! He felt like he was going to cry. His father was going to be so angry! And what was Len going to say?

"Hmm," Len said neutrally, upon arriving at the scene.

"Oh, Lenny," said Carl, no longer able to hold back the tears. "What am I gonna do? Pop is going to kill me!" Carl's shoulders shook with the violence of his sobs.

Carl's brother reached into his canvas bag and pulled out their father's hand drill. He handed it to Carl and said, "Two holes."

"What?"

"Drill two holes in the top of the deer's head, in the spots where antlers would be."

Carl was confused.

"Just do it," said Len, agitated as it had started to snow.

Carl's cold fingers could barely hold onto the drill handle as he cut through the fur and bone into the warm skull. There was little blood.

"What now?" said Carl, trying to hide his shaking hands. "Don't we have to gut it?"

Carl's brother reached into his bag again and pulled out a small pair of antlers. At the base of each antler was a screw shank sticking out.

"Twist these tight into the doe's head," said Len, his eyes darting nervously across the laurel thicket. Something about it didn't feel right to Carl, but he did as his brother instructed.

"There you go, little brother. Shot yourself a four-point on your first opening day of buck season." Len slapped Carl on the back. "Now let's get this thing gutted so we can take it back to the truck. Won't Pop be thrilled?"

"He's going to know it's not a real buck, Lenny. I can't lie to Pop."

"Who do you think taught me this little trick, Carley? Our daddy and his brothers have been doing this for years." Len laughed.

"It's not right, Lenny," said Carl. "I didn't hit the deer I was aiming at. I got the fever, and I shook and couldn't stop. I shouldn't have pulled the trigger and taken the shot. What if it had been you or Pop I shot at?"

"But it wasn't," said Carl's brother. "It wasn't. You shot a doe instead of a buck. The meat isn't going to go to waste. And you can't eat antlers."

Wiping the tears from his cheek so his brother wouldn't see, Carl reached into his sheath and pulled out his buck knife. It was a gift from Pop for Carl's twelfth birthday. The deer antler handle fit neatly in his hand. *That's right. You can't eat antlers.*

"What do you say you show me how to gut my first deer?" Carl said to his brother, trying to smile.

"Got one last thing to do before we do," answered Len, reaching into his canvas bag once more to pull out a rosary. Taking his younger brother's hands, the two men knelt in the bloody snow to pray.

I Drive Myself Sane

Ice flies off the semi ahead of me
a near miss. I feel targeted,
reminded of risk and how we rode the run of
parking lot curbs as kids, a tightrope pedaling
that passed as daredevilry in a southwestern PA
small town. I imagine a near miss for yesterday's
rural bike rider, a rock that could have catapulted him
into oncoming or ongoing traffic. I'm commuting,
already late to my latest adjunct gig—
it is a gig, that du jour word for lovely
transient itinerancy, the show-up-and-perform
status of a part-timer. Like an Uber driver
for myself. On the road
I marvel at what's hill-built, those
who live and walk on a tilt, where snow and rain
are always moving, never staying plain.
And the hillsides some inhabit can be so tenuous,
shifting then sliding to almost allow no escape,
splintering selves as they lose their shape.
My next risk is to grope for a misplaced
chocolate bar, then unwrap it like I'm
in a Starbucks instead of a crowded interstate.
I bless the mess as it melts in
my mouth, and hope my mind drifts
as my chassis stays straight, blemished
but still burning rubber.

Karen Ferrick-Roman, Ed.D.

Ghostprints in the Snow

The driveway is empty of snow. But there's plenty of snow in the yard, with four more fresh inches piling up this January afternoon in Western Pennsylvania.

The puffy flakes lead me on a walk down memory lane—more specifically, on the mile or so hike through fallow fields to get to the Big Hill of childhood. Mount Misery, we called it. Lore had it that a hunter felled by a heart attack rolled down the hillside to the very bottom. Dead, of course. (It was hardly surprising, even as a kid, that no one could ever provide a name or date for the unfortunate event. But then, as now, it was a great story leading to a superior, slightly scary name.)

Mount Misery provided my first and only flights in an old-school, wooden toboggan with a curled front and a bottom rubbed with sticks of wax—leftovers from summer, when the neighborhood ladies used wax to seal their homemade elderberry and strawberry jellies. Only two runs, and we were exhausted.

Closer to home, we also trudged paths through the snow. Just out the yard and into the woods, we'd cross into the pasture where Dad gave a great run on skis made from barrel staves, where I eventually learned to avoid barbed wire fences when I was sledding, even if the Flexible Flyer's metal steering mechanism was stiff or frozen. But before I learned to strongarm the steering or roll off, as older siblings screamed out their advice, bright red drips started falling from the super thick, rose wool pink mittens Aunt Mary knitted—a startling punctuation on the white-covered ground. My older sister escorted me away from the pasture, into the woods, and back home. Five stitches crisscrossed the top of my left thumb. I never knew how many were in the eyebrow.

In time, both the five-stack snowman in our yard that melted into a rideable snow pony and the shock of the scars faded.

Generation to generation, the joy of playing in the snow lived on with my own kids. But dressing for the occasion changed drastically. Our kids never had to endure what they consider a grievous indignity: slipping bread bags over feet before sliding on boots, a '60s and '70s thing that was just the way it was when it was snowy and you wanted to play outside and didn't have waterproof, Thinsulate boots good to -20 degrees—and it didn't matter because nobody else did either.

Instead, we wore woolly clothes that grew mini snowballs from baby snowflakes until the moment we went inside. Then the little balls turned into tiny rivers on the kitchen floor. Mom grimaced when she walked through the puddles and got her slippers wet as she was trying to get us to hang our so-wet, snow-wet gear on the clothesline in the basement. And one of us usually hid a snowball in a pocket or under a tassel cap to get in the last word of the night after we were all dried off and drinking Swiss Miss or Ovaltine.

These hot drinks gave way to fair-trade cocoa for our kids. Marshmallow creme stepped aside for the real, live, rectangles of extruded sugar and gelatin. But when our sons were young, the wagon wheel shape of Fox and Geese remained a generational carryover, keeping alive a tag-playing tradition.

Our yard in the infinitely more civilized suburbs also persisted in bearing tell-tale tracks of the resident snowball army. In years past, the hedge of snow piling up now at the edge of the driveway and the yard would have been conscripted for the wall of a fort, on either or both sides of the driveway. The driveway itself gained a new purpose as a line of demarcation for teams battling for snowball supremacy.

Depending on the players, the adult driveway shovelers might be merely moving targets, like the ducks on the spinning wheels at the summer carnival—until the shovelers emptied an entire load of snow in the direction of the attack. With luck, it would look like a mini-blizzard and distract, if not disarm. Laughter was guaranteed.

Then there was the time of enchantment, somewhere around a wintry 2 a.m., that my husband and I zipped up jackets, found our gloves, and walked around inside the silent embrace of a snow globe that transformed our block. Under that waxing moon, life was soft, magical. Ours were the only footprints. Even rabbits, raccoons, and birds were sleeping. By morning, the evidence of our escape into fantasyland would never be suspected. Sleeping kids and chatty neighbors would never know about our secret walk, taken as our sons hibernated, home alone for those 15 otherworldly minutes.

In time, our boys and their man-child friends created a tradition with two workshop floodlights and a football. The snow went bonkers, breaking into all sorts of patterns, curly whirly snow angels of running backs, heralded by shouts and laughter. Only three hard rules: No blood. Take your boots off at the door. And nobody stays in wet clothes inside.

In their ever-advancing age, the boys would coordinate efforts to transform the white hedge of snow piled next to the driveway into a misshapen igloo, the best one big enough for four. The two women who would become daughters-in-law ensured their icy hut had a roof that didn't leak—at least while they were inside.

One winter's day, when the kids were away at college, we were dismissed early from work because of the heavy snow. My husband and I took stock of the pantry and the liquor cabinet, then sent emails and texts around the oval loop that was our street. Footprints filled the driveway, and our living room contained one of the finest Blizzard Parties on record. Most everybody came, simply because reruns on TV were the only other option (nobody was streaming anything back then except fishermen). Besides, we could tell snow stories, embellishing like those stereotypical exaggerating anglers.

These years, the numbers have changed drastically. A portion of those once-visiting neighbors, even some of our family members, curl up somewhere around 27 degrees latitude in Florida, light years away from Pittsburgh's 40-degree location. At least they have the courtesy not to rub in the 70-degree temperatures while I'm layered in Thinsulate, Smartwool, and Cuddl Duds under my parka. The warm widow stands alone.

A growing hedge of white 18 inches deep intersects at the edge of the driveway and the lawn, just like in the old days. But this year, the yard and the driveway show no signs of life. No tire tracks. No footprints. No surprise snowballs shattering on the ground next to me, bouncing off my back or smacking my glasses, leaving annoying bits of frostiness to drip, drip, drip. Vacant, sterile, powdery snow. With more to come.

Shovel is put to pavement, and the payload is pushed into the yard. Scoop, rinse, and repeat for 30 or more feet. Mechanical, mundane movements battle this vacant, sterile, powdery snow. The air fills with flakes floating groundward.

More ghostprints.

More shoveling.

Hunting With My Old Boyfriend

Dark, except for the snowlight.
We head down the road when
a coyote lets out a long howl—
Its pack joins in yipping like hyenas
with a few barks. We stop.
We stare. They sing to us, wishing us luck
on our hunt, hoping for guts
and field dressing remains.

You tell me that in cultures
where the people and ravens know
one another, the ravens dip and roll
showing their bellies
over the places the deer were hiding
so the hunters knew where to go.

It is strange how much I still know
the etchings of your face, how much I still adore you
how I once fell in love with you
in a deer blind, so many years ago.
We sip hot water and wait
quietly.

Two ravens come, gunk-gunk loudly
I watch them fly over
no tipping or belly shows
but they are so close together—
it is as if
they are holding hands.

Naming/Not Naming

—the active enchantment reaches my dust—
Ralph Waldo Emerson

Almost evening
the pond reflects returning green

Overhead, two ducks
fly too high to name

Ripples of wind
a cascade of dancing light

Evening—green—
two ducks

A cascade of words
the silence between words

all things named and unnamed
eternally dancing

high on the iridescent ripples
of a duck's green wing

While at Eyecare Associates, My Dead Mother Walks In

The glasses are off.
And my dead mother walks in.

Yes, my mother.

She's short, busty. She wears a gray cardigan or jacket.
She wears sensible gray shoes.
Her blouse is red. Her pants are white.

She sits across from me. She looks a bit lost.

I try not to stare.
But without my glasses, I can hardly tell if I am staring.

She has glasses, and, I think, a ruddy complexion.
She sits. I sit, taking blind side-eye glances in her direction.

Yes, the spitting image.

But then a man in a yellow tie hands me my new glasses.
The lenses are bright, perfectly clear, and made of a high index plastic.
The frame is a rigid, bright blue titanium alloy.

I try them on.
And, no. No. It is not my mom.

I say, thank you, to the efficient man in the yellow tie.

He leaves.

And then I take my glasses off, again.
And sit for a while.
Staring.

Monongahela Rye

Day after day we built
these sloops and schooners,
built them for the ocean
though it's two thousand miles by water
to the sea.

Built them up to the deckhouses,
finished the hull, put them
in the water, filled them
with casks and jugs
of whiskey,

or stacks of lumber,
for the men, just the men,
to take downstream. Not a single one
of those ships ever came back.
Just the men and the money.

All along the river,
paid for everything
with Monongahela rye
whiskey.

At New Orleans
sold the lumber and bought
masts, yards, cordage, sails,
fitted the ship out for sea,
paid what else was needed
in whiskey.

Sailed to Havana
or Savannah
or France
sold the ship
and the rest of the
whiskey.

Took passage to
Philadelphia,
walked over the
Alleghenies,
carrying the money
home.

My Old Man and the Sea

Before re-lighting one of his Marsh-Wheeling cigars, my dad would grip the densely packed stogie in his big, sun-stained hand and, with a powerful tap, beat the cold ash from the end. I held that hand while he died. By then, though, it was frail and had turned both the color and temperature of that powdery ash.

When he was alive and vibrant, my dad's hands defined him. He was a worker, and his hands showed it. They were calloused and strong. His entire frame was commanding. Flesh, blood, and hardened bone that spoke a narrative of a life spent providing.

His body, those hands, had a time, place, and function. At ease with the facts of life and temporal death, I was comfortable in the knowledge that the continuum of my dad's bodily time, place, and function had its stretch, and it was now over.

So, there in that room, in the midnight stillness of death, I was fixated not on his hands but on the thought that the best parts of my dad had nothing to do with his tangible existence. I was locked in on the idea that the finest thing he'd offered up was swirling around in the mist and wooded hollows of my youth and that it was alive and well in the chambers of my memory.

When I was very young, my dad and I found precious common ground hunting in the woods of western Pennsylvania. We were at ease there with nothing more than the untamed landscape around us and the odd pleasure of each other's company to sustain us. Our backs against huge oak trees, our feet on the damp leaves, we talked very little. It was silent time—like we were alone together, each deeply comforted by the fact that the other was there.

He was good at hunting. His steadiness and stoutness allowed him to wait quietly for hours in the gray misery of late November for deer he somehow knew would appear. His alertness and uncanny ability to remain collected made it so that he could see antlers, straight lines, cupped ears, and, calmly—like he was going to wipe a spot of mustard from the corner of his mouth—raise his weathered rifle and shoot straight every time.

My dad was free in those woods, liberated to be himself and emotionally at ease. His enjoyment existed regardless of environmental conditions. His well-being was fortified by self-confidence and, I think, a quiet resignation that he was not in charge—an acquiescence to be a subject of the land, the woods, God. Out there, with an unpressured but resolute approach to his task, his brain was at peace.

I loved hunting with my dad. I loved being with someone who appeared so completely in control in a wilderness over which he had none. Although I never felt his equal, I was, through the magic of some impalpable osmosis, able to feel confident and capable there with him— in the presence of his confidence and ability. Those were delightful and satisfying times. But they floated by like swiftly moving clouds and were long ago swallowed by the curve of the earth.

My father was a complicated man whose Germanic lineage gifted him with a penchant for strict methods and high expectations. He was prideful, judgmental, and infinitely stubborn. When I was a child, I accepted that. But by the time my adolescence closed up shop, I had tired of it. I became unwelcoming. He dug in. We grew distant. Although we spent time together, our conversations grew to be uncomfortable. Eventually and regrettably, stubbornness, a trait we undoubtedly shared, led us to a guarded place where we found a new silence, antithetical to that which we shared in the woods. We didn't want that. But neither he nor I could seem to find the words or the actions or the time to fix it. And then, too early in the arc of our relationship, he became both old and sick.

About the time my dad turned 65, Alzheimer's disease swooped in with a tailwind and began its hellish attack on his mind. It nibbled around the edges of his day-to-day life like a rat at a cheese wheel, consuming bits of his memory and pieces of his ability. Each sunset carried with it the gravity of knowing not just that the rat had more and he had less, but that the feeding would never end.

After seven grueling years of battle, the disease planted its flag in his brain. His mind was, from that point on, in permanent captivity, rendering him unable to enjoy the memory of those good times in the woods while simultaneously putting any hope of us talking about them in the grave.

Alzheimer's doesn't have the decency to simply take the life of its victims; it first tortures them by stripping away their ability to know they ever had one. This, while it crushes the world of those with whom the patient is close, those who care, those who seek in vain the answers to untold numbers of questions.

I tried to imagine the way he must have felt each day during that secluded time. Was he scared? Lonely? Lost? Was he all those things? Was he none of those things? Did he understand the way things were going, the way so much was escaping his cognition and recollection? Or was every day just a hazy assembly of non-descript, indiscernible moments and occurrences stacked on top of one another like a heap of cubed potatoes? The wondering about these things was relentless, and the answers evasive. The empty chasm of my dad's life near the end kept me up at night, testing my intellect for a profound understanding, searching my bedroom for a security blanket of clarity and emotional respite. For months, I tossed and turned.

One night after hours of restlessness, I decided to read, thinking I would either escape into the story or bore myself to sleep. Not wanting to start something new, I reached into my stack of "already-reads" and pulled out a copy of Ernest Hemingway's "The Old Man and the Sea." In that narrative, Hemingway tells the story of Santiago, a forgotten fisherman, and his battle with a mighty fish alone on the ocean.

Santiago is a thin and sinewy man, meagerly clothed and always barefoot. His skin is abnormally dark and deeply crevassed from the piled-up influence of salt, sun, and wind. His hands are scarred and thickened from the years of handling ropes, lines, and the oars of his skiff. He presents as a man who has known great toil.

Santiago's journey into the ocean seems unnecessary. His age and diminished capacity are akin to someone ready for cool drinks under shade trees. But he goes fishing. He continues with his life on the water, indifferent to the world's view of it. And he does it alone.

When he hooks into the fish, it becomes his in-the-flesh adversary. Out there in that desolation, though, there are greater things at play. Santiago's identity, the life that justified him, and the work that forged his outward appearance were ending. The talents and skills that defined his life were leaving him, slipping away like smoke through a clasping hand. I think he knows that, but Santiago never lets on. He holds with confidence the tether that binds him to a fish from the abyss.

As I leafed through the dog-eared pages of my copy of "The Old Man and the Sea" that restless night, I came to a passage I had underlined in my first read. It was at a point in the story when the hooked fish was steadily pulling Santiago into a wilderness of water and a shadowy unknown.

Here, Hemingway deftly slid in two sentences to foreshadow Santiago's coming days and forlorn moments. Hemingway writes:

"He looked across the sea and knew how alone he was now. But he could see the prisms in the deep, dark water and the line stretching ahead and the strange undulation of the calm."

After reading that collection of words, I re-read them. And then again. The words grew heavy with parallel metaphor. Thoughts of my dad and his plight flooded my brain, and for the first time since his diagnosis, I found, through the eyes of an imaginary man and the words of he who created him, an avenue for understanding.

Santiago's life as it was materially known was ending; he was alone, and he "knew how alone he was." But he could "see the prisms in the deep dark water and the line stretching ahead." This tired old man, engaged in a personal battle so large that what remains of his earthly life may be consumed by it, recognizes at once his place in the ocean and in the world. He acknowledges the overwhelming swirl of natural beauty into which he was being steadily pulled and the mystery of that which lay ahead.

Santiago, the fictional character, engaged in a physical contest, and my very real dad, in his languid condition, I reasoned, may have a great deal in common. What lies ahead for each is daunting. But they both may see a comforting light mingling, like an old friend in a room full of strangers, with the darkness that surrounds them.

They have, after all, been there before. Santiago, the well-seasoned fisherman, and my dad, the hardened man. They waited confidently in places that were wild and over which they had no authority, places where they'd known a singular order and had been successful—Santiago on the waters of the Gulf Stream and my dad in the woods of the Allegheny Plateau. Each of those men was content when they released themselves to the rhythm of the earth and the warm decree of providence. Each of those men saw peace in the "strange undulation of the calm."

Becoming untroubled by my father's situation, finding that same tranquility, was, until that night and my rediscovery of that prose, an impossible task. Until then, I'd forgotten about the mutual assuredness my dad's presence delivered to our days in the woods. Until then, I'd not appreciated the understated value of my dad's intrinsic life. My thoughts were consumed by the historical power of his hands, by the physical contributions of his body, and by the sternness of his voice. Hidden in the shadows were the lessons of his mind and the beauty of his silence.

A week after beginning to re-read "The Old Man and the Sea," I came to its final pages. There Santiago, upon returning to the land after his epic battle, is having a conversation with a caring and compassionate young friend—the only character in the novel who knows Santiago as more than a fisherman. Hemingway notes: "He noticed how pleasant it was to have someone to talk to instead of speaking only to himself and to the sea."

I was pleased that Santiago's lonely journey had ended and warmed that he had someone with whom to share both the story and his time. Simultaneously, though, I was wrecked by thoughts of my father, forever alone, endlessly adrift. Despite my acquired empathy and rationalized view of his situation, I was fully awake to the truth. He would never know Santiago's pleasant reflective satisfaction and closure—not in this world. My old man would, instead, remain at sea.

For some time on the night he died, I sat in silence with my dad. Internally, I decried the cruelty of the disease that was claiming him and the condition it had wrought upon his body. Repeatedly, I rued the brevity of our time together while I reminisced, alone, about our hunting days and wished for things not possible.

Yet there we were, alone together in a time and place when the clock stood still and the world was as big as the woods. And the shifting breeze and the rustling leaves and the unspoken words of my dad's placid mind swirled around us. There was a strange undulation lurking in that calm—invisible, untouchable, but still more powerful than the earthly realities of brawn, bone, and the fading ashen flesh of my father's dying hand.

Poem for the Doe with the Crumpled Leg

After the trail-hike I drive away as if in a different
story—gravel popping along Penny Lane, I burrow
deeply in my thoughts, & perhaps because I burrow
deeply, I miss the way sunshine spills through trees,
slides across a scrim of sky & perhaps because I miss
the shine across a scrim of sky, I don't notice the small doe
with the crumpled leg, & two others flanking her in woods
beside the primitive road, until the dogs press their panting
bodies with tense delight against the window glass,
but don't crater our silence with barking, not yet,
not even once, their quiet concentration & em-dash
tails a palpable astonishment, how the doe
with the crumpled leg keeps grazing even when I stop
the car, her wild stillness no ordinary light, wakes me
from remembering's daze—winter, Valentine's Day message,
the friend with groves of tumors blooming in her lungs
couldn't catch her breath. Collapsed. EMTs unable
to revive—but now I'm spellbound by springtime doe
with crumpled leg, the angular swerve of her disfigurement,
hairpin curve of ankle joint, scar-tissued skin & bone
never to touch ground again, a weird wrecked wing
mimics curl & lobe of sideways question mark—
what makes some things last, while others can't be saved?
I watch the doe bend & brace her body on three legs,
the long reach of her neck, ears flickering messages
I can't comprehend, soft purse of her lips pulling gently,
the tender tufts of grass.

Moving into Mamaw's House

Three whitetail bucks misty-eyed hanging
In the living room. The recliner still.
Boxes filled with another man's treasure.

Is this life? Cleaning up after the dead.
Breathing in dust made of her bits and pieces
From decades past.

Overwhelming. Mom keeps saying *overwhelming*.
Too many syllables. Too weighty. Underwhelming, if anything.
Six dressers. Three beds. Eight spatulas. One body.

Is this life? Preparing this old house for my eventual death.
Six bookshelves. Three pairs of boots. Eight water bottles. One body.
Acquiring possessions. Too many syllables. Too weighty.

Outside the living room window
A robin nest forming. A comforting place.
The recliner rocks and, misty-eyed, I watch.

This is life.
I had never watched someone die before that day, but
I've watched a buck bleed out.

This is life.
One body made of her body and mom's and mine
And this house and that buck and all that we've ever known.

This is life.
Overwhelming.
A comforting place.

BIOGRAPHIES

Stacy Alderman – Nonfiction

Stacy Alderman's writing has been featured by *THEMA Literary, Kelp Journal, LoveNotes!* (71st Street Books, 2024), and more than a dozen others. She was the recipient of the Children of Steel Fiction Award (Anaphora Literary, 2024) and frequently writes freelance articles for a local newspaper. She lives near Pittsburgh with her husband and two defiant rescue dogs. Find her online at StacyAldermanWriter.com.

Mischelle Anthony – Poetry

Mischelle Anthony's recent work has appeared in *Autofocus, Naugatuck River Review, The North (UK), Cimarron Review, and Little Patuxent Review*, and in her chapbook, *[Line]* (Foothills Press). She grew up in Oklahoma, now lives in Scranton, Pennsylvania, and teaches at Wilkes University.

Roy Bentley – Poetry

Roy Bentley is the author of *Walking with Eve in the Loved City*, chosen by Billy Collins as finalist for the Miller Williams Prize, *The Trouble with a Short Horse in Montana*, chosen by John Gallaher as winner of the White Pine Poetry Prize, and *Boy in a Boat* selected for the University of Alabama Press.

Rachel Berryman – Poetry

Rachel Berryman is a sustainable energy technologist and writer based in Berlin, Germany. A native of Tioga County, NY, her written work explores philosophical themes and reflects on her country of origin with the distance and perspective of years spent away. Her poetry has appeared in *OPEN, Beyond Words, Sunday Mornings at the River*, and other outlets.

Angela Cannon-Crothers – Poetry

Angela Cannon-Crothers is a naturalist, educator, writer and wildcrafter. Her most recent book *Changing Seasons in The Finger Lakes* won the Cayuga Lake Books Award for Creative Prose in 2019. Her other books include *The Wildcrafter, Our Voices, Our Wisdom; An Herb Haven Year, and Grape Pie Season* (illustrated by Darryl Abraham). She works as the Head of Forest Schools.

Gary Ciocco – Poetry

Gary Ciocco teaches philosophy, writes poetry, and reads print magazines. From 2005-2017, he helped run the First Friday Poetry series in Gettysburg. He teaches for Carlow University and WVU. He has published poetry in anthologies as well as *Pittsburgh Quarterly, Backbone Mountain Review*, and *Rune*. He reviews poetry and philosophy books for the *Pittsburgh Post-Gazette*.

Todd A. Comer – Poetry

Todd A. Comer is a poet, scholar, and native of West Virginia, though he now lives in Yellow Springs, OH. He is currently circulating two collections, one focused on Marietta, Ohio, *Mary and Etta: Appalachian Poems*, as well as a second currently entitled, *My Life as a Rug: Poems*.

Jessica Cory – Poetry

Jessica Cory is the editor of *Appalachian Journal: A Regional Studies Review*. She is also the editor of *Mountains Piled upon Mountains: Appalachian Nature Writing in the Anthropocene* (WVU Press, 2019) and the co-editor (with Laura Wright) of *Appalachian Ecocriticism and the Paradox of Place* (UGA Press, 2023).

Shaheen Dil – Poetry

Shaheen Dil was born in Bangladesh and lives in Pittsburgh. Her poems have been widely published in literary journals and anthologies and nominated for the Pushcart Prize. She has published three collections of poetry: *Acts of Deference* (Fakel 2016), *The Boat-maker's Art* (Kelsay Books 2024), and *Letters to My Younger Self* (Gyroscope Press April 2025). https://shaheendil.com.

Theresa Doerfler – Fiction

Theresa Doerfler is a fiction student in Carlow University's MFA in Creative Writing Program. She has a BA in English from Notre Dame and an MA and PhD in English from Ohio State University. She works as an adjunct professor at Carlow, a freelance writer at *National Catholic Reporter*, and a Literacy Pittsburgh volunteer.

Ziggy Edwards – Poetry

Ziggy Edwards edits the online zine *Uppagus*, among other things. Her poems and short stories have appeared or are forthcoming in publications such as *5 AM*, *Dreams & Nightmares*, *New American Writing*, and *Strange Horizons*. Pittsburgh Poetry Exchange published her first chapbook, *Hope's White Shoes*, in 2006.

Timons Esais – Poetry

Timons Esaias is a satirist, writer and poet living in Pittsburgh. His works, ranging from literary to genre, have been published in twenty-two languages. Honors include half a dozen Best of anthology appearances, a Winter Anthology Award, two Asimov's Readers' Awards, the Louis Award, an Intrepid Award, a SFPA Prize, and numerous award shortlists.

Karen Ferrick-Roman – Essays

Living in Greater Pittsburgh keeps Karen Ferrick-Roman grounded in neighborliness, arts and ethnic culture, do-it-yourself traditions, and practical thinking that rises to untangle problems. She relishes deadlines—a hangover from newsroom days—and surprised everyone (including herself) by completing her doctorate in education at Duquesne University at an age when others plan retirement. She invests time in family, horses, dogs, and cats.

Bradley Firchow – Fiction

Bradley Firchow is a medical student in the Rural Physician Leadership Program at the University of Kentucky and a creative writer focused on Appalachian narratives that subvert expectations. His work explores the emotional landscapes of place, memory, and identity. He was raised in Kentucky and West Virginia and writes frequently about coming of age in rural spaces.

Keegan Flanagan – Poetry

Keegan Flanagan is an MFA student at Carlow University, writing poetry that embodies a romantic, lyrical tradition in a modern, contemporary voice. Son of a widowed, immigrant mother, Flanagan's work reflects the struggles and small joys of childhood in a working-class home, and gives voice to the universal experiences of love, loss, and longing.

Daniel Flatley – Fiction

Daniel Flatley is a reporter and writer living in Maryland. A former Marine and graduate of Columbia University, his nonfiction has appeared in *Bloomberg*, *Time Magazine*, and the *Washington Post*. His fiction and poetry have appeared in the *Northern Appalachia Review*.

Jane Ellen Freeman – Fiction

Jane Ellen Freeman lives south of Shepherdstown, WV. Jane has published short stories in the *Northern Appalachia Review*, the *Anthology of Appalachian Writers*, *Florida Writers Anthologies*, and The *Ghosts of Shepherdstown Vol. I*. Other publications: *Beyond the Stone Eagle Gate* (YA), *The Whispering Chimney* (MG), and two others. Website: www. janeellenfreeman.com

gaye gambell-peterson – Poetry

Artist/poet gaye gambell-peterson centers herself with memory of roaming mapled hills in 1950s Wellsville, NY. Her chapbooks (*pale leaf floating*, and *MYnd mAp*) combine her collages & poems. Other published sites include *American Journal of Poetry: Vol 5, qarrtsiluni* (Fragments), *Erase/Transform, Persimmon Tree, Northern Appalachia Review*, and three anthologies, including *Flood Stage: an Anthology of St Louis Poets.*

Donna Geise – Poetry

Donna Geise's writing is imagery-rich, filled with autobiographical details and events from her small childhood town, and often alludes to writers and pieces she admires. Her poetry manuscript titled *Searching for a Song* is slated for publication in the fall of 2025. She lives in Huntsville, surrounded and inspired by Alabama's northernmost part of the Appalachian foothills.

J.r. Gill – Poetry

J.r. Gill teaches AP Literature, British Literature, and World Literature at McClain High School in the village of Greenfield, Ohio, along the border of Midwestern cornfields and the Appalachian foothills. He is a lonely hunter, hiker, writer, and heathen. He is a student of the late great Dr. Hunter S. Thompson.

Richard Hague – Non-Fiction

Richard Hague is Poet Laureate of Cincinnati and the Mercantile Library. A member of the Southern Appalachian Writers Cooperative and Writers Association of Northern Appalachia, he has published 23 books and chapbooks, and hundreds of poems, essays, reviews, and stories in such journals as *Creative Nonfiction, Poetry, Appalachian Journal, Iron Mountain Review, Cincinnati Review*, and *Alabama Writers Forum*.

Dodi Hanes – Literature of the Outdoors and Environment

Dodi currently lives in western New York and is writing a middle-grade chapter book series. She has articles published in *Organic Family Magazine* and a local journal, *Parental Guide Magazine*. Recently, her poetry was published in *The Last Stanza Poetry Journal, Moonstone's World Environment Day 2024, Yawp Magazine*, and *Sweet Smell Journal.*

Tori Hirsh – Poetry

Tori Hirsh is a multimedia designer, writer, and artist based in Pittsburgh, PA. She graduated from Carlow University in 2019 with a BA in Media Arts, received a certificate in Applied Mythology from Pacifica Graduate Institute in 2023, and returned to her alma mater in 2024 to pursue an MFA in Creative Writing with a specialization in poetry.

Mary Pat Hyland – Fiction

Mary Pat Hyland is a writer from New York's Southern Tier. She's a graduate of Syracuse University and an award-winning former newspaper journalist. In 2013, she was selected as Arts Center of Yates County Artist in Residence. She has previously been published in the *Northern Appalachia Review*. When not writing, she enjoys gardening and cooking—especially Italian food.

Janet E. Irvin – Poetry

Janet E. Irvin is an educator, poet, and the author of eight mystery/thriller novels under the name J.E. Irvin. Her poems have appeared in *Hawaii Pacific Review*, *Creosote*, *The Raven's Perch*, *Sky Island Journal*, *Flying Island Journal*, and *Lothlorien Poetry Journal*. Irvin resides in southwest Ohio, on the edge of a nature park, which serves as inspiration.

Sandi Johnson – Poetry

Sandi Johnson. Cross-genre writer who is a Liberian-born English professor. M.F.A. student at Carlow University. Published works appeared in *Sounds of this House* with the National Book Foundation, *Solstice Literary Magazine*, *Carlow MFA 20th Anthology*, and *Watershed Journal*. Awards include: 2009 Solstice Institute for Diverse Voices Prize and the 2021 Stephen Dunn Poetry Prize in *Solstice: A Magazine of Diverse Voices*.

Jessica Jones – Poetry

Jessica Jones (MA, University of Montana) is full-time faculty at Kent State University-Stark, where she teaches place-based writing, Native

American Literature, and poetry. She comes from a long line of makers and musicians in Eastern Ohio and Western Pennsylvania. Her writing has appeared in numerous journals and anthologies, and her book *Bitterroot* (Finishing Line Press, 2018).

Mark Sebastian Jordan – Poetry

Mark Sebastian Jordan lives in the central highlands of Ohio. He comes down from the hills to raid the cities for culture, by and by.

Alexandra Kemrer – Poetry

Alexandra Kemrer's poems have appeared in *Voices from the Attic*, Pittsburgh City Paper's "Chapter and Verse," and *Rune*. She is a member of Carlow University's Madwomen in the Attic program. Her debut chapbook, *Mill Spit* (Finishing Line Press, 2019), is based on childhood experiences in a steel mill town on the Monongahela River. She lives and works in Pittsburgh, PA.

Gail Langstroth – Poetry

Raised under the Big Skies of Montana, Gail Langstroth lived, studied, and worked in Europe for 38 years. Making her home in Pittsburgh now, Langstroth is a tri-lingual lecturer, international eurythmy performer, translator, poet, and visual artist. Langstroth's poetry books, *Firegarden* (Get Fresh Books, 2020), and *Ghost Friends—in Praise of Jean Valentine* (Lefty Blondie Press, February 2025), are both bilingual, Spanish and English.

Cathy Lentes – Poetry

Cathy Cultice Lentes has lived in the Appalachian foothills of southeast Ohio for over 35 years. A recently retired educator, she writes for both adults and children. Lentes is the author of a poetry chapbook, *Getting the Mail* (Finishing Line Press, 2016), and co-author, with Wendy McVicker, of the epistolary collection, *Stronger When We Touch* (The Orchard Street Press, 2023).

Jeremy Lloyd – Poetry

Jeremy Lloyd grew up in Indiana County, Pennsylvania, and lives in East Tennessee, where he teaches on the faculty of Great Smoky Mountains Institute at Tremont. His poems have appeared in *Gray's Sporting Journal* and *Still: The Journal.* He is the author of *Forest Time: Footnotes to an Outdoor Education*, forthcoming from the University of Tennessee Press in 2026.

James Lowell – Poetry

James Lowell currently writes from a remote, two-mile island in the Atlantic's stream. Short- and long-listed for Fish's 2024 poetry prize, his work has appeared in *Canadian Literature, Caribbean Writer, English, Fortnight, Fourth River, Gramercy, L.A. Review, Martha's Vineyard Times, Milk House Review, O Miami, Orchard Poetry Journal, Sandy River Review, Southern Florida Poetry Journal, Texas Poetry Review.*

Nancy McCabe – Poetry

Nancy McCabe is the author of nine books, most recently the middle grade novel *Fires Burning Underground*, the YA novel *Vaulting through Time*, and the comic novel *The Pamela Papers.* Her work has appeared in *Michigan Quarterly Review, Prairie Schooner, LARB, and Gulf Coast,* among others, received a Pushcart, and made notable lists ten times in Best American anthologies. She has lived in northern Appalachia for nearly 25 years.

Sharon Fagan McDermott – Non-Fiction

Sharon Fagan McDermott is a Pittsburgh-based poet and essayist who teaches Environmental Literature at Winchester Thurston School. Her recent books include *Life Without Furniture* (Jacar Press 2018), a book of poetry, and *Millions of Suns: On Writing and Life* (University of Michigan Press 2023), an essay collection named one of *Poets and Writers* Magazine's "Best Books for Writers."

Kerry McGee – Poetry

Kerry McGee's first publication was in the Grade 8 section of the Montgomery County Public Schools' 1987 Superintendent's Writing Awards anthology; she has since grown up and become a much more nuanced writer. Kerry writes across genres, and her work has been featured in a variety of publications, including *Highlights for Children, Spider, and Ladybug magazines.*

Martha G. Michael – Poetry

Martha G. Michael is a professor emerita, an artist, and a writer living in Columbus, Ohio. She has published her poetry and artwork for the cover with P*udding Magazine: The Journal of Applied Poetry*, and poetry with the *Northern Appalachia Review, The Ohio Bards Anthology*, and her artwork and poetry at Steinbecknow.com, and *The 2024 Paw Paw Anthology*.

Linda Mills Woolsey – Poetry

Linda Mills Woolsey grew up in Lawrence County, Pennsylvania, and currently divides her time between Allegany County, New York, and a place on French Creek in Crawford County, PA. She's a retired educator whose poems have appeared in *The Sow's Ear Poetry Review, Coal Hill Review, The Windhover, About Place, Northern Appalachia Review*, and other journals.

Mayson Moffitt – Literature of the Environment and Outdoors

Mayson Moffitt is a writer from northern Appalachia whose work explores memory, family, and regional culture. Raised in the Ohio River Valley, he draws on personal experience to reflect the layered identity of the region. "Echoes of Home" focuses on the small, grounded details that reveal something larger—how gravel roads, family stories, and quiet inheritance form the rhythm of a place.

Ben Moyer – Essays

Ben Moyer's writing about nature, outdoors, and conservation issues appears in numerous regional, state, and national publications. He is a winner of the Outdoor Writers Association Enduring Excellence Award, honoring a lifetime body of work. Moyer's book, *Smoke to See By: Knowing Nature in Northern Appalachia*, was the Writers Conference of Northern Appalachia's Book of the Year in 2023.

Aaron Murphy – Fiction

Aaron grew up in the Daniel Boone National Forest of Kentucky and spent much of his life scrambling up coal-filled hills and driving down mountain roads for hours on end, coming up with stories as he fell in love with Appalachia. He now lives in Savannah, Georgia, with his wife and German Shepherd, where he studies History and English.

Karen Whittington Nelson – Poetry

Karen Whittington Nelson lives in Southeast Ohio on a small farm. Her work has been published by or is forthcoming in *Rattle, the Anthology of Appalachian Writers, Women Speak, Sheila-Na-Gig Online, Thought I Heard a Cardinal Sing: Ohio's Appalachian Voices, Pine Mountain Sand & Gravel, Gyroscope Review, Main Street Rag*, and various journals and anthologies.

Ed Pfeifer – Essays

Ed Pfeifer is a business owner, freelance writer, and father of two young adults. His work has appeared in *The Mountain Journal, Trib Total Media's* regional newspapers, *Gun Dog Magazine*, and *Gray's Sporting Journal*. Ed makes his home in Western PA with his wife, Stacey, and Ginger the beagle.

Olivia Plummer – Poetry

Olivia Plummer is currently in her junior year at Westminster College in western Pennsylvania. She is twenty-one years old and a natural-born

Pennsylvanian. Her work reflects the potential complexities within the relationships we develop with ourselves, our families, and nature. She has a specific attachment to flowers, namely lilies, which can often be seen littered throughout her work.

Molly Prosser – Poetry

Molly Prosser is the author of the poetry collection *Rubbernecking* (2015). Her poems appear in *Pittsburgh City Paper, Split Rock Review, So to Speak Journal*, and more. She is the winner of the Lefty Blondie Press 2025 Editors' Choice Broadside Series. Molly holds an MFA in Poetry and is currently pursuing her MSt in Creative Writing from Cambridge University.

Maddie Ratcliff – Poetry

Maddie Ratcliff is an Appalachian poet who believes in the magic of tradition and rural living. She is always searching for and writing about places where nature, spirituality, and the eternal converge. She holds an MFA in Creative Writing, Poetry from Bowling Green State University, and resides in southern Ohio.

Margaret Kasper Reed – Poetry

Margaret Kasper Reed is an educator and teacher living in Pittsburgh. She has published in numerous journals and anthologies, including *Poet Lore, The English Journal*, and *Rattle*. Her chapbooks include *Children of the Sky* and *Lament's Grocery*. With pianist Gwen Beckman, she collaborated on the theatre piece *Into Blue*, which incorporates Gershwin's Rhapsody in Blue with poetry and art.

John Repp – Poetry

John Repp is a writer, folk photographer, and digital collagist living in Erie, Pennsylvania. In December 2025, Sheila-Na-Gig Editions will publish his sixth collection of poetry, *Never Far From the Egg Harbor Ice House*.

Amy Le Ann Richardson – Poetry

Amy Le Ann Richardson's full-length poetry collection is *Out of Places*. She has also published two chapbooks: *Make Believe Worlds We Built Together* and *Who You Grow Into*. Her work has appeared in *Pine Mountain Sand & Gravel*, *Still: The Journal*, and other journals. She writes, grows food, and advocates for her community and the environment in Carter County, Kentucky.

Susan Sailer – Poetry

Susan Shaw Sailer has published four books of poems—*On The Doorstep*, *The Distance Beyond Sight*, *The God of Roundabouts*, *Ship of Light*—and two chapbooks, *Bulletins from a War Zone* and *COAL*. Sailer lives in Morgantown, West Virginia, and is a member of the Madwomen in the Attic program of Carlow University.

Fred Shaw – Poetry

Fred Shaw is a Visiting Lecturer in Creative Writing at the University of Pittsburgh and was recently named to the Advisory Board for the International Poetry Forum. His first collection, *Scraping Away*, was published by CavanKerry Press in 2020. A second book is in the works.

Ed Simon – Poetry

Ed Simon is Public Humanities Special Faculty in the English Department of Carnegie Mellon University, as well as the Editor of *Belt Magazine* and the forthcoming *Pittsburgh Review of Books*.

Helen Collins Sitler – Non-Fiction

Helen Collins Sitler has lived all her life in Western Pennsylvania. She is a Pushcart nominee. Her creative nonfiction has appeared most recently in *Beautiful Things*. Other flash nonfiction has appeared in *Post Road*, *Hippocampus*, and *The Sunlight Press*. Longer essays have appeared in *Harmony*. Her craft essay appears on the *Brevity* blog.

Juanita Smart – Poetry

Juanita Smart's work has appeared in *About Place Journal*, *River Heron Review*, *West Trade Review*, and *Cirque*, among others. She finds joy in the company of other writers and nature enthusiasts. She drafts her best ideas for poems while exploring local, northwestern Pennsylvania game lands "off leash" with her galumphing dogs, Eliot and Wilson.

Annabelle Smith – Poetry

Annabelle Smith is a writer and poet from western Maryland and an undergraduate student at Franklin & Marshall College. She has received national recognition from *Scholastic Art and Writing* for her work in poetry. She has been published in *The Foundationalist*, *Philadelphia Stories*, *Black Coffee Review*, and other journals.

Lois Spencer – Fiction

Lois Spencer's short stories have appeared in *Northern Appalachia Review* Volumes 3, 4, and 5; *PMS&G* Volume 2,6 and in two Ohio Writers Association anthologies: *House of Secrets and Should This Book Be Banned?* Her work has also been published in *Persimmon Tree*, *Anthology of Appalachian Writers*, *Women Write*, and other journals. Raising two sons, teaching students ranging in age from junior high to post-retirement, traveling, reading, and paying attention provide the fodder for her stories.

Andi Stout – Poetry

Andi Stout is an Appalachian writer from West Virginia now living in central Pennsylvania. She is the author of Pushcart-nominated "Tiny Horses Don't Get A Choice." Her poems have appeared in *One Art*, *Cardinal Anthology*, *Mulberry Literary*, *Still: The Journal*, and many other journals, magazines, and anthologies. Andi earned her MFA degree at West Virginia University.

Matthew Ussia – Poetry

Matthew Ussia is the director of Duquesne University's First Year Writing Program in spite of the fact that he got a C- in freshman writing and was rejected from Duquesne's MA program. He is also an editor, scholar, podcaster, post-doom thereminist, and softcore punk. His first book, *The Red Glass Cat*, was published by Alien Buddha Press in 2021. www.matthewussia.com.

Sandra Vrana – Poetry

Sandra Vrana, a daughter of a coal miner, grew up in western Pennsylvania. After earning a PhD in Literature and Cultural Criticism from Indiana University of Pennsylvania, she taught classes at Alderson-Broaddus University of West Virginia for decades, becoming a Professor of Literature and Writing. She was a member of the Barbour County Writers for more than twenty-five years.

Arlene Weiner – Poetry

Arlene Weiner is active in community poetry groups in Pittsburgh. Her poems have been published in a variety of journals and anthologies, and read on Garrison Keillor's *The Writer's Almanac*. Arlene was awarded a MacDowell Fellowship. She also writes plays. Ragged Sky Press published three collections of her poetry: *Escape Velocity* (2006), *City Bird* (2016), and *More* (2022).

Caroline Wermuth – Poetry

Caroline Wermuth coordinated the Lee Bennett Hopkins Award for Children's Poetry, the Public Poetry Project, and the Lynd Ward Graphic Novel Prize for the Pennsylvania Center for the Book in the Penn State Libraries. Her poems have appeared in *Northern Appalachia Review*, *Frogpond*, *Heron's Nest*, *World Haiku Review*, *Haiku Girl Summer*, and in the *New Jersey Botanical Gardens* (NJBG).

Rodd Whelpley – Poetry

Rodd Whelpley is the author of *Blood Moon, Backyard Mountain* (2023, Broadstone Books), and three chapbooks. He grew up in Geneva, Ohio, in Ashtabula County. www.RoddWhelpley.com.

Stefanie Wielkopolan – Poetry

Stefanie Wielkopolan is a native Michigander who now calls Pittsburgh, PA, home. Up until the age of eight, she spent every Saturday watching cartoons at a bowling alley bar. She credits this experience with instilling in her a love of good dive bars, people-watching, and writing poetry. Her chapbook, *Home is a Sweater*, was recently published by Finishing Line Press.

Christine Wolfe – Poetry

Christine Aikens Wolfe's poetry books are *Mary McDermott Wolfe* (Main Street Rag, 2025) and *Garlanding Green* (Dos Madres Press, 2018). Her poems appear in *Gargoyle, Paterson Literary Review*, and more. Her fiction appears in *The Wild Hunt* (Air & Nothingness Press) and *Rune*. Christine is president of the Pittsburgh Poetry Society and a Madwoman in the Attic.